CHALK, CHALLENGES, AND CELEBRATIONS

TALES FROM THE TEACHING FRONTLINES

ACHAMMA ALEX , BIBIN SEBASTIAN

Contents

Contents

Foreword

Teaching is more than just a job; it is a lifelong commitment to shaping minds and touching lives. As you go through the pages of *Chalk, Challenges, and Celebrations: Tales from the Teaching Frontlines*, you will come across stories that reflect the heart and soul of education. Teaching is about much more than delivering lessons from a textbook. It is about nurturing growth, encouraging curiosity, and fostering resilience. Every classroom is a world of possibilities, where each child comes with unique needs, dreams, and challenges. A teacher's role is to guide them through those challenges, helping them discover their potential.

This book gives us a glimpse into the many facets of teaching—the joys, struggles, and triumphs that define a teacher's journey. Every story in this collection speaks of the deep connection between teacher and student, and the immense responsibility that comes with this role. Teaching is not only about imparting knowledge; it is about inspiring students to think critically, to ask questions, and to explore the world around them. It is about building confidence in the uncertain, providing guidance in the unknown, and sparking a passion for learning that will last a lifetime.

The stories within these pages highlight the many challenges that teachers face daily. They speak of the ever-evolving needs of students, the diversity of backgrounds in every classroom, and the need to adapt teaching methods to make education relevant to all. These stories also shine a light on the dedication, perseverance, and compassion that teachers bring to their work. They show how teachers go beyond the curriculum to help students navigate life's difficulties, providing support not just academically, but emotionally and socially.

Teaching is also a journey of learning. As much as teachers shape their students, they too are shaped by their experiences in the classroom. Every student teaches the teacher something new—about life, about growth, about humanity. These stories show that no two classes are the same, no two students are alike, and each teaching experience is unique and deeply personal.

What resonates most in these stories is the sense of fulfillment that comes with being an educator. There is joy in seeing students succeed, in witnessing their growth, and in knowing that, in some small way, the teacher has contributed to their development. The book reminds us that teaching is not always easy, but it is always rewarding. It is filled with moments of triumph, moments of learning, and moments of pure joy that make the challenges worthwhile.

As you read this book, remember that teaching is more than just a profession. It is about shaping the future, one student at a time. Every teacher has the power to make a lasting difference, not just in the classroom but in the world. Let the stories in this book inspire you to appreciate the hard work and dedication that teachers put into their craft, and the profound impact they have on their students' lives.

Fr. (Dr.) Saju MD CMI
(Principal, Rajagiri College of Social Sciences)

Setting The Tone ....

Teacher: A Vocation with Vision and Re-vision

"Did you understand?" This may be the most frequently uttered words by a teacher in her/his entire teaching career. Whether s/he gets an answer "yes" or not s/he repeats the question for enormous times. The teacher's earnest desire to make the student understand is well reflected in that perennial genuine question. Interestingly, we don't often hear the question from the students, "Teacher, did you understand me?"

What is education then? Making the student understand or understanding the student? As a teacher, mostly I have strived to make my students understand through my lessons and tested their understanding through the exams. But, in that process, I miserably failed to understand them.

Usually, what we understand or come to know about a student is only the tip of the iceberg. Regarding teaching, it's said: "In order to teach John Latin, you should know both Latin and John." As teachers most of us know "Latin," but to what extent we know John? "John"'s personality, family background, interests, success, failures, aspirations, hurdles of life...as teachers our knowledge is limited. Why a student is distracted? Why s/he is reactive than pro-active? Often we don't understand them or misunderstand them. The great teachers must trust them when they are abandoned as worthless and useless. May be the small phrases like, "don't worry", "It's ok", "no problem", "try again" etc might touch their hearts and will make them feel that they are being understood.

Our knowing of the students is often limited to our seeing. But a teacher must have visionary seeing in order to understand them. The question, "how many seeds are there in an apple?" can be easily answered by cutting the apple into the pieces and counting the seeds. We need only sight for that. Simple act of "seeing" will help to complete this task. But to answer the question, "how many apples are there in an apple seed?" we need the visionary seeing. Only this visionary seeing of the students will give a teacher the correct understanding of "Johns." •

Often the teachers are addressed as "respected teacher" and they really like to be addressed so. But, the great teachers always respect the students! The word, "respect" comes from the Latin words, *"re(again) and spedere (see)"* together means "to see again". The teachers need to respect- see the students again and again. "Why does s/he behave in such a way? Why did s/he respond so? Seeing them again sometimes will change our perceptions about them. Will make the teacher more understanding, sympathetic and connected to the students.

A teacher with vision and re-vision will make the students to join Alexander the great in acknowledging that, "I am indebted to my father for living, but to my teacher for living well". And such teachers can truly celebrate their vocation as a teacher.

Fr. Benny Nalkara CMI
(Provincial and Manager)

Editors' Note

As we reflect on the remarkable experiences captured in *Chalk Challenges and Celebrations: Tales from the Teaching Frontlines*, it becomes clear that teaching is much more than a profession—it is a profound calling. The narratives within these pages unveil the joys, struggles, and triumphs faced by educators as they navigate the complexities of shaping young minds. Each story sheds light on the deep, emotional bonds between teachers and students, and how these relationships transcend the classroom to impact lives in profound ways. The contributors share personal insights that resonate with the essence of what it means to be an educator in an ever-changing world, revealing the heart and dedication that this vocation requires.

This collection not only celebrates the victories but also highlights the challenges teachers encounter, from adapting to evolving educational methods to balancing emotional connections with academic responsibilities. The book stands as a testament to the resilience, empathy, and passion that drive educators to persevere despite the obstacles. As readers journey through these pages, they will gain a newfound appreciation for the role of teachers as both guides and lifelong learners, reminding us all of the immeasurable impact educators have in shaping the future.

Editors

Contributor Acknowledgemnt

Dr. Shanthi Simon completed her MA from Marthoma College Tiruvalla (1994), followed by an MPhil (1995) and PhD (2001) from Mahatma Gandhi University. She served as a Professor in the Department of Humanities and Social Sciences at Puducherry Technological University, and retired on April 30, 2024.

Dr. R. Sudha, a retired Professor of French and former Head of the Department of French at Madurai Kamaraj University, served for 36 years. She completed her M.A., M.Phil, and Ph.D. in French from the same university and received the French Government Scholarship three times. Dr. Sudha co-authored two French textbooks and has 21 publications. She supervised 8 Ph.Ds and 26 M.Phils, with 4 Ph.D. projects still in progress upon her retirement in November 2021. She was Registrar in charge of Madurai Kamaraj University.

Dr. K.S. Krishnakumar, hailing from Orumanayoor, Trichur, is a renowned poet, critic, and educationist. He currently teaches at S.N.M. Training College, Moothakunnam, and contributes regularly to magazines and journals. His major works include *Extra Thakkol*, *Neelasharikal*, and *Self-talk*. He has received multiple honors, including the Best Educationist Award and the Rashtra Vibhooshan Goldstar Achiever's Award.

Dr. Sudha G is an Associate Professor in Political Science at S M Govt. First Grade College, Kollegala, Karnataka. Her interests include writing stories, poems, and articles, as well as singing. She actively conducts workshops on gender sensitization and women's empowerment and is dedicated to social service, focusing on supporting students and women.

Dr. Achamma Alex, Professor and Head of the Department of Languages at RCSS, holds an MA from St. Berchmanns' College and an M.Phil. and Ph.D. from the University of Kerala. Beginning her career in 1987 at Mar Thoma College for Women, Perumbavoor, she later served Christian College, Chengannur, as Head of the

English Department and Principal until her 2020 retirement. She has presented numerous papers at national and international conferences and has served on the University of Kerala's Board of Studies.

Dr. Marie Pierre Augustin is a retired Professor of French with a distinguished career spanning over three decades. He served at the Dept. of French, School of English & Foreign Languages, and was awarded the UGC Emeritus Professorship from 2015 to 2017. With nine Ph.D. students mentored, six books authored, and numerous conference papers and chapters, he has significantly contributed to French and Francophone studies.

Dr. Sheila Elizabeth Abraham joined the English Department at Mar Thoma College, Tiruvalla, in 1980 and retired as Head in 2009. She holds B.Ed., M.Phil., Ph.D. degrees, and a Postgraduate Diploma in Counselling. She has been a member of the Board of Examinations for M.A. English at Mahatma Gandhi University. Post-retirement, she taught in the Self-financing M.A. English Programme at Bishop Kurialacherry College, Amalagiri, for 15 years.

Dr. Shaleen Kumar Singh is the Associate Professor and Head of the English Department at Swami Shukdevanand Postgraduate College, Shahjahanpur, U.P. A poet, critic, reviewer, and translator, he has edited over two dozen books on literature. His poetry collection *Proprietary Pains* was published by Poets Printery, South Africa, and *From Home to House* on Kashmiri Pandits was published by HarperCollins. He also publishes with Sahitya Akademi and runs the online journal *creativesaplings.in* (ISSN 0974-536X).

Dr. Seema Bhaduri, based in Nashik, Maharashtra, completed her M.Phil. on 'Time in Five Novels of Salman Rushdie' and her Ph.D. on 'A Comparative Study of Six Indian Stream of Consciousness Novels.' She authored *A Dynamic Modernity: Adaptation and Parody in Six Twentieth Century Indian Novels* (2022) and has published research articles, short stories, and a travelogue. Her interests include reading, writing, and engaging in socio-cultural activities.

Dr. Rincy Saji is an Assistant Professor of English in the Department of Languages at Rajagiri College of Social Sciences (Autonomous). She holds a Ph.D. in English Language and Literature from Mahatma Gandhi University, Kerala. Her research interests include cultural studies, film studies, war studies, posthumanism, and literary theory. She earned her postgraduate and undergraduate degrees from St. Teresa's College, Ernakulam, and Vimala College, Thrissur. Rincy qualified for the UGC NET in 2018 and secured UGC-NTA NET with JRF in 2020.

Dr. Kavitha Gopalakrishnan is an Assistant Professor at the Department of English, Baselius College, Kottayam, Kerala. She has been the review editor of the international refereed journals WEC (Writers Editors and Critics) and IJML (International Journal of Multicultural Literature) for a decade. She has to her credit publications in several national and international journals and edited books. Her research interests are Cultural Studies, Popular Fiction, Indian Literature, and Poststructural theory and literary criticism.

Dr. Pradeep P N, Assistant Professor at Rajagiri College of Social Sciences, Kerala, coordinates the Centre for Entrepreneurship Development and Innovation (CEDI) and manages the RCSS_Gyan Prayag Incubation Centre. He holds a PhD in Social Work from TISS, Mumbai, with a specialization in Social Entrepreneurship. With over a decade of industry experience, he is a skilled trainer and mentor in social enterprise, entrepreneurship development, and project management, and serves as the Nodal Officer for RCSS_IEDC.

Dr. Unnikrishnan P. is an esteemed Assistant Professor in the Department of Philosophy at Sree Sankaracharya University of Sanskrit, Kalady, with over 25 years of dedicated teaching experience. His major areas of expertise include Indian Philosophy, Logic, and Research Methodology, where he brings a wealth of knowledge and a passion for deepening philosophical inquiry. Dr. Unnikrishnan has contributed to the academic community through numerous published book chapters, advancing the study of philosophical perspectives and methodologies. Renowned for his commitment to education and scholarship, he continues to inspire students and colleagues in his pursuit of philosophical understanding and critical thinking.

Dr. Jacob Alias, Assistant Professor of English at Rajagiri College of Social Sciences, has over 5 years of teaching experience and 4 years of research experience. His PhD research delves into the struggle to preserve a romantic temperament amidst pain, mortality, and metaphysical turmoil, with a focus on displacement and identity affirmation. His areas of expertise include research methodology, diasporic studies, and gender studies. Known for his dynamic teaching style, Dr. Alias inspires critical thinking and intellectual curiosity.

Allen Antony is an Assistant Professor of English in the Department of Languages at RCSS. He holds a Master's degree in English Language and Literature from Sacred Heart College, Thevara, and a Bachelor's degree from St. Berchmans College, Changanacherry. His academic interests include historiographic metafiction and regional literature.

Alex K.O is an Assistant Professor of English at Rajagiri College of Social Sciences. He holds a B.A (Hons) and M.A in English Literature from The English and Foreign Languages University, Hyderabad. He has volunteered with the United Nations Development Programme on a project related to SDG14 (Life Below Water) and has presented papers at various conferences. His poems have been published in online journals from India and America.

Dr. Sony G is an Assistant Professor at Rajagiri College of Social Sciences. She is a poet, short story writer, and critic, with a PhD in Malayalam Language and Literature from Mahatma Gandhi University, focusing on Kavisiksha. Dr. Sony has published poetry, short stories, and research articles, and has presented papers at national conferences. A top graduate in Malayalam, she has won numerous awards in literary and cultural festivals, including accolades for her poetry and performances.

Navami. T. S. is an Assistant professor of English at Manipal University Jaipur, Rajasthan, and is currently pursuing her PhD at the Department of Humanities and Social Sciences, Indian Institute of Technology (IIT) Kharagpur, West Bengal, India. Her research is rooted in literary urban studies, gender studies, cultural studies, and authorial intention and interpretation in literary criticism.

Prof. Varghese S Nedumthallil is an experienced educator with a career spanning over five decades. He holds degrees in Zoology, Education, and Malayalam Language & Literature from Kerala University. He served as a lecturer and professor at St. Peter's College, Kolenchery, and as Principal of St. Mary's College, Thuruthiply. He has also coordinated distance education for Madurai Kamaraj University. His hobbies include reading, writing articles, and watching sports. He continues to contribute through teaching and academic engagements.

Dr. Sujeesh C.K. is an Associate Professor of English at Sree Sankara College, Kalady, and the Coordinator of Renaissance: Centre for Research, Extension, and Learning. He is actively involved in academic and research initiatives, fostering creativity and engagement among students. With a focus on literary studies and educational development, Dr. Sujeesh continues to contribute to both teaching and research.

Jithin John is an Assistant Professor at Postgraduate Department of English and Centre for Research, Baselius College, Kottayam for the last eleven years. His major areas of interest are Theatre Studies, Cultural Studies and Film Studies. He pursues his research in "Theatre Studies" under Mahatma Gandhi University, Kottayam. He was born as the son of Mr. John Joseph and Ms. Susy John. His spouse is Hanna Paul and Ninav John Paul is their only son.

Aishwarya Paulson is an Assistant Professor of English in the Department of Languages. She graduated from Pune University and cleared the NET (2018) and Maharashtra SET (2016). She has worked as a Lecturer at Narayana Hrudayalaya Paramedical College, Bangalore, and as an Assistant Professor at Kristu Jayanti College,

Bangalore. Actively involved in organizing international and national conferences, she has also won awards for creative writing at state and inter-collegiate levels.

Dr. Joji John Panicker is an Assistant Professor in the Research Department of English at CMS College, Kottayam, and Director of the Internal Quality Assurance Cell (IQAC). He coordinates RUSA and the UGC Paramarsh Scheme at the college and is a Research Supervisor at Mahatma Gandhi University. He has served on the college's Governing Council, Academic Council, and Board of Studies. Dr. Panicker is also the Joint Secretary of GIEWEC and Associate Editor for *Writers Editors Critics* and *Literary Oracle*.

Vijesh P.V is the Librarian at Rajagiri College of Social Sciences (Autonomous), Kalamassery. He is dedicated to facilitating access to a wide range of academic resources and ensuring the smooth operation of the library. His role includes managing collections, supporting research, and enhancing the learning experience for students and faculty.

Vishnudas A V is a Library Assistant at Rajagiri College of Social Sciences (Autonomous), Kalamassery. He plays a key role in supporting the daily operations of the library, assisting with resource management, and ensuring that students and faculty have access to necessary academic materials.

Suryagayathri is a Library Assistant at Rajagiri College of Social Sciences (Autonomous), Kalamassery. She assists in the daily functions of the library, ensuring efficient access to academic resources and providing support to students and faculty in their research and study needs.

Sada Warsi, a Research Scholar in the Education Department at Integral University, thrives in independent living while pursuing her passion for writing. Her work encompasses articles, research papers, and book chapters, all underscored by a strong commitment to research and academic exploration.

Dr. Susan Sanny, with an MA in English, B.Ed., MA in Sociology, M.Phil., and PhD in English, is the Principal of Nitte International School since 2023. She previously served as an

Assistant Professor at Kristu Jayanti College for 16 years and has 12 years of experience in various educational institutions. Her academic interests include Indian Literature, Subaltern Studies, Gender Studies, British Literature, and Translation Studies.

Surya P. Nair, an Assistant Professor of English with the Collegiate Education Department (Government of Kerala), holds a Master's degree in English and a Bachelor's in Education from Kerala University. After teaching for over 14 years in Central schools across India, she joined Government College Nadapuram and now works at Central Polytechnic Trivandrum. A part-time PhD researcher, her interests include Cultural Studies, Translation Studies, and Literatures of marginalized communities, with a focus on pedagogy and cultural hybridity.

Dr. Madhumita Chanda, with over 20 years of teaching experience, is a faculty member in the Department of Humanities at Heritage Institute of Technology, Kolkata. She has published works in translation, including short stories, poems, and the Bengali autobiography of Jayanta Mahapatra. Currently, she is translating Mahapatra's autobiography into English for a Sahitya Akademi project. Her specializations include Translation Studies, Indian Literature, and Functional Communication Skills.

Shoma Elizabeth Francis is an Assistant Professor of French in the Department of Languages at Rajagiri College of Social Sciences (RCSS). She holds a postgraduate degree in French from Madurai Kamaraj University and has nine years of teaching experience in government and non-government institutions. Previously, she worked as a Lecturer at Government Arts College and All Saints' College in Trivandrum, as well as a PGT at Trivandrum International School.

Dr. Jeena Shaji is an Assistant Professor of English in the Department of Languages at RCSS. She holds a PhD from Mahatma Gandhi University, specializing in women's narrative and feminist film theory. She earned her MA from Calicut University and a BA from MG University. A scriptwriter of award-winning short films on women's issues, she also contributes to Onmanorama as a podcast creator. Dr. Jeena has published in Scopus-indexed and UGC-approved journals and is an active digital content creator.

Dr. Bibin Sebastian is a researcher and educator specializing in cultural studies, English literature, and posthumanism. He holds a PhD in English from Nagaland Central University and has published extensively on various topics. He earned first rank in his post-graduation at Central University of Haryana and received the Kerala Higher Education Scholarship for his undergraduate studies.

Thomas A Mattappallil is an Assistant Professor in the Department of Languages, Rajagiri College of Social Sciences, Cochin. He holds a BA in Journalism, Political Science, and English, an MA in English with Communication Studies, and an MPhil in English, and is currently pursuing a PhD in English. With eight years of teaching experience, his research interests include comparative, American, postmodern, and lockdown literature.

Dr.Aswathy Balachandran is an Assistant Professor of English at Mar Athanasius College(Autonomous) Kothamangalam. She is a bilingual writer who has published poems in both online and print journals. Her poem collections include *Contours* (English), *Aparichithar* (Malayalam) and *Koode* (Malayalam).

Keerthana Deepak is a first-year B.Sc. Psychology student at Rajagiri college of social sciences. With a deep passion for writing, she enjoys crafting stories and articles that reflect her thoughts and experiences. An avid reader of classic literature, Keerthana finds inspiration in the works of great authors. In addition to writing, she expresses her creativity through painting and loves playing table tennis.A keen traveler, Keerthana enjoys exploring new places and cultures, enriching her understanding of the world around her.

CHAPTER ONE

A Lifelong Calling

Shanthi Simon

One's profession can be a choice or destiny. For some, the career path is a winding road of exploration and discovery. For others, it is a straight line, clear from the very beginning. Born into a family of teachers, for me, teaching was a choice—or rather, a calling and a source of profound fulfilment that seemed predestined. As I reflect on my experiences as a teacher, what stands out for me is the immense gratitude I feel for the unparalleled privilege of participating in one of mankind's most exhilarating occupations. I recall with pride and fondness, my beloved grandfather and parents who motivated, guided, and set examples for me in this noble profession. These early influences were not just familial expectations but living examples of the profound impact a teacher can have. Their legacy became my inspiration, driving me to carry forward the torch of education with the same passion and dedication.

My teaching career began in 1995 with a brief stint at Women's Christian College, Chennai where I first experienced the thrill of standing before a class, the nervous excitement of preparing for the daily poetry sessions and the joy of connecting with students. The journey concluded with my retirement from Puducherry Technological University in 2024 after 23 rewarding years. From my first class on Gerard Manley Hopkins' "Pied Beauty" to my last one on professional ethics, the richness and variety of experiences I have gathered have shaped me profoundly. I have experienced moments of ecstasy and anguish, happiness and sorrow, excitement and despair, hope and helplessness. Each class was a new adventure, each student a new challenge and opportunity. Being in a technological institute, I had to find ways to make language and literature relevant in a technology focussed environment. As I look back on this journey, I realise that my EXPERIENCE can be encapsulated in ten words:

- Engaging
- eXciting
- Poignant
- Explorative
- Rewarding
- Inspiring
- ExperiEntial
- Nourishing
- Challenging
- Emotive

No other profession could have been this engaging. As a friend, philosopher, and guide, sharing ideas and engaging in discussions with students has opened new vistas and unravelled varied perspectives. It has been a journey of continuous growth and learning, with each interaction contributing to my personal and professional development. As a language teacher, the additional responsibilities of literary and theatre clubs at the institute provided immense opportunities to engage in and promote literary pursuits. The freedom to facilitate creative talent in students and witness their diverse modes of expressions was indeed a blessing. While I was trying tirelessly to engage the students in various activities, I found myself engaged by their questions, perspectives and growth.

The exciting moments during lively class discussions and other activities have gifted me a treasure trove of memories. The lasting relationships I have built will forever be part of me. Seeing the impact of our work continue through the lives of our students is deeply gratifying, as is the joy of contributing meaningfully to society directly or indirectly.

There have been poignant moments too — moments that touch the heart deeply. It has always been miserable to witness students struggling because of challenging backgrounds and limited resources, yet seeing their remarkable resilience was heart-warming. During the pandemic, seeing students grappling with isolation, loss and uncertainty was heart wrenching, leaving lasting impressions. It also brought moments of incredible resilience and feeling of togetherness.

Teaching has made me more explorative on all fronts. While encouraging curiosity and critical thinking in others, I have continuously explored new methods, approaches and technologies to enhance effectiveness and reach out to every student. I am proud to say that my journey into technology—be it smartphones, laptops, or applications like WhatsApp— was initiated and navigated by my children. It has provided fun-filled moments of learning that will always remain fresh in my mind.

The rewards of teaching are manifold — often unexpected and immeasurable. From a student's success story to a simple 'hello 'message years after graduation or a note sharing how a difference was made in their life, these rewards are treasured for a lifetime. These moments of recognition make life worthwhile, and I consider myself immensely wealthy in this aspect.

It is heartening to know that we have inspired someone through our thoughts, words, or deeds. Igniting a lifelong love for learning is truly fulfilling. Similarly, I have been inspired by my students' creativity, resilience, and fresh perspectives.

In a way, this is what experiential teaching is all about. Experience has always facilitated learning which was rich and powerful. Diverse experiences contributed to holistic learning and created an environment that prepared me for challenges.

Education nourishes the mind, body, and potential. As I look back, I am grateful for the emotional support and guidance I could provide, which in turn nourished my senses. I have found my own intellectual and emotional growth deeply nourished by my experiences in and out of the classroom. Whether helping a student navigate personal challenges, or guiding them in career decisions or simply lending a listening ear, these moments of connection have been deeply satisfying.

Of course, this came with challenges too – adapting to diverse learning needs and keeping up with evolving standards. These challenges, though daunting at times, provided opportunities for growth and innovation. Integrating technology into my teaching was one of the biggest challenges I faced. I struggled and still struggle to find meaningful ways to incorporate digital tools. The continuing support of my students pushes me to evolve and experiment new possibilities.

My teaching experience has been intensely emotive, taking me through a full spectrum of emotions—joy at students' achievements, frustration with systemic limitations, disappointment at failures, hope for the future, and empathy for struggling learners. This emotional investment is what made teaching a calling, a calling that touched my heart and soul. It was a mixture of pride and sadness to watch students leave the institute every year to move on in life, reinforcing the profound emotional bonding that this profession created.

My career as a teacher has been a beautiful tapestry of experiences—rich, varied, and deeply fulfilling—a journey of continuous growth, learning, and inspiration. As I turn the pages of my life's book, moving from the chapters of active teaching to the new adventures that lie ahead I do so with a heart full of gratitude. I feel blessed for the privilege of having been a teacher with countless students who have enriched my life and for the colleagues who have supported and inspired me along the way. and with excitement for the new adventures that lie ahead in this lifelong calling. I carry with me a wealth of experiences, memories and relationships that will continue to nourish and inspire me. These experiences have coloured my life in the richest of hues. To all teachers and educators, I say: cherish the moments of connection and never undermine the profound impact you have on the lives you touch. In shaping the minds of others, we ourselves are shaped, learning and growing in an endless cycle of shared discovery.

• 5 •

CHAPTER TWO

A Teacher Muses

R. Sudha

A new batch of students of M.A. French steps into the Department. They are a little scared of me. Let it be. Classes in full swing. Days roll by. Students slowly drawn towards me. A subtle rapport develops, the teacher rolls into a confidante, a counsellor. I would call these two years a 'relationship building' program, done through a pure methodology of observation, analysis and inference. By the end of the two full years, the batch is ready to take wings, most of them rolled into teachers. Race is relayed! A candle lit, it would light more.

On every 5 th of September, I think of my own teachers, who have tutored and tailored me. I fondly remember Rev. Sr. Maria of Holy Cross Convent, Thuthookudi, who taught me to whisper a prayer for the souls in danger, at the bell of the fire engine, now replaced by the siren of the ambulance. A prayer on my lips every time I hear the siren. How a good thing taught early in life becomes a habit! I think fondly of my school teachers who helped me

develop the love for words, insisting on using the dictionary, reading the newspaper and books. As my thoughts travel to St. Mary's College, Thuthookudi, I am grateful to the teachers who sharpened our analytic literary skill through debates and seminars in our B.A. English major classes. How indebted I am to Professor Rajeswari Chandrasekar, who brought alive the characters of

French Literature in our M.A. French classrooms at Madurai Kamaraj University. I am equally indebted to Monsieur Bruno Mègre, Director, Department of Evaluation and Certification, France Education International, Paris for his dynamic classes, which I attended as a French Government scholarship holder. If I have been able to perform well in my profession, I owe it to all of them and I bow to the teachers who have inspired me.

If September 5 is a day to celebrate teachers, I think equally of my students, who have made me enjoy this sweet sailing, with happiness and pride. Small and finer things touch me. A past student called me after a gap of 5 years. "Ma'am just wanted to know how you are doing". Happy. A student walks in with a gift, "For you ma'am, with my first salary." Overwhelmed. A student offers analytical and critical feedback about my classes.

Appreciated and points integrated into my classes. An alumnus comes in and says 'Ma'am, I want to sit in your class and listen to you. Your class is magical. You begin with a word and then go on to explain many things. At the end of the two-hour class, the board is full of words. How much I have learnt in your class!' Kudos, Sudha. Another alumnus says, "Ma'am, we don't like to miss your classes, because your class is packed with vocabulary." Wow! A note of thanks comes from the HR division of a school, expressing their happiness over the excellent performance of one of their teachers who was a former student of our Department. Let me call it a day. What more does a teacher want! To see her students

perform well, and to wish that they perform better than her!

I have been lucky to have taught in a school, a college and the university. Teenagers, adolescents, adults. Richer by this versatile experience. "Men may come, men may go, but I go on forever." I have gone on for 34 years in the university. 3 full decades. Well, I have gone a long way in my career - teaching. You really don't feel old if you love what you do. Well, with every academic year, new admissions, new faces, younger than the yesteryear. I go up one year in age and I meet a batch one year younger. O my God, the gap keeps widening! Spirit is electrified, though flesh is weak. But I have always tried to keep up with the times, dancing to Batchmates.com, Orkut, FB, WhatsApp... If not, you are lost in the game! It is not just enough to keep up with the race. I have to keep myself updated and give my maximum to my students, who are a budding team of teachers or translators.

My Department and my students are always my priority. My device – the brilliant ones need to be guided and the weaker ones have to be taken well care of and nourished. When I realize that a student has problems at the home front, I counsel and render the financial or emotional support needed. As a teacher, I would consider this as an achievement - the Golden Jubilee Celebrations of The Department of French that I organized in December 2020, a year before my retirement, with the help of my team. I was able to bring together alumni from the very first batch of 1970. Creation of a WhatsApp group of the alumni of the Department of French, MKU followed suit. It is a platform for posting job opportunities, the senior Alumni Professor Rajeswari Chandrasekar and Professor Marie Pierre Augustin, (both of them are former Heads of the Department), offer free online NET coaching classes. Mr. S. Jeyakar, Head of the Department, FA Indian Private School, Kuwait takes a lot of initiatives in organizing online seminars for the benefit of our alumni. Mr. Alexis Kittery who lives in France, takes care of the French connection. Our group also shares online French newspapers, journals, books and other pedagogical materials. The group is indeed alive and kicking.

Life is a lovely and continuous process of learning. At every stage of life, we need something – an institution, people and memories - to pave the way to blossom forth into wholesome human beings, the backdrop of course, the home. My profession itself has been an institution of learning for me. I emphasize to my students that they should make an assessment about themselves at the end of every year spent in the department, both in their academic and personal fronts. They should always nurture the child in them and remain curious in the quest of knowledge. Above all, remain an empathetic human being.

The meaning of my profession continues – having brought together the alumni for the golden jubilee celebrations, keeping them linked through our WhatsApp group for professional enrichment, staying connected with the students of yesteryears and new alumni of the latest batch. The bliss, contentment and pride of having done something good and useful for my Department and my students. What more would I ask for!

Thanks for this center stage, O Lord!

• 9 •

CHAPTER THREE

There is No Change without Change and No Sweetness

K. S. Krishnakumar

Whenever I am asked to think about my teaching career, the first name that comes to my mind is that of Narayanan Master from Kalpetta. Greek philosophers have stated that "No man ever steps in the same river twice, for it's not the same river and he's not the same man," and this is true in the case of teaching. Each and every student sitting in the classroom is unique. The signature recorded in the attendance register by a teacher on the day of joining will be quite different from the last signature he puts on it on the day of his retirement. Two or three shady trees in an open space for students to assemble together, with a playground on one side of the building, is the landscape common to all schools, but the teachers who reach there to teach students are quite alike. We may come across a reserved student in the school of a really talented speaker-student. Every classroom in a school has its own weather condition. The lady colleague of Narayanan Master, who was well renowned for his cultural contributions, never felt anything odd in such a variety, till date.

The urge to learn and teach is inherent in every human being from the day of his birth. This urge has its manifestations in different games and role-play activities even before a child goes to school. The child is even capable of enacting the role of a teacher invariably with a book on his right hand, a cane on his left hand and with spectacles over his nose. It is quite natural for young children to make use of these role-playing sessions that give them the opportunity to exhibit their capability to express what they know and to create the impression of being a Mr. Know-all. Every conversation that gives instructions may not be teaching, but the taste and smell and shape of teaching is visible in all types of communications where man communicates with authority. The classical ideology of teaching as a teacher-centred process is the root cause of all such thoughts and outlook. This concept of teaching is evident in all spheres of human activity from a newsroom to the scintillating word of films. Rarely do we come across heralds and directors with more expertise than a teacher!

But times have changed. All societal enterprises including teaching have become humanist in their approach. Now they are child-centred and experiential in their outlook. Teaching has slowly drifted away from the status of an individual-controlled process to a more democratic nature. Every process connected with education has become polyphonic. Projects with socialist points of view are slowly foregrounded. Slogans celebrating children as producers of knowledge resound across society. Primal matter in the process of learning has become prominent whereby society has come to realise that the process of dictating and taking down notes and information alone cannot give good results. Constructivism has overhauled behaviourism due to its increasing relevance and fame. Students get more opportunities to discover facts and make presentations in classrooms.

Discussions are still going on regarding the replacement of traditional methods of addressing students from the front part of the class, with novel techniques and methods. The seating arrangement in classrooms has undergone a revolutionary change.

The primacy of a teacher is thus re-written in every sense. However, it is true that this ideological stance, even now, is hardly reflected in the educational sphere. The real outlook of those who design the modern curriculum for teaching is not fully transferred to the implementing sectors. It is a known fact no other sector is as vibrant as the education sector in terms of suggestions for improvement. Reformations, their failures at the implementation level and rethinking are often repeated in a cyclic way in the education sector. Therefore, it is quite meaningless to stick on to any particular curriculum or teaching methodology. However, a firm theoretical foundation and background is a prerequisite, and most often a necessity for teachers to deliver the curriculum effectively. The field of education envisages timely revision and there is perhaps no other field that is binding to consider and apply these timely changes. Changes that come across in this world and human lives influence the classrooms, the most. The ever-changing learning-teaching process reminds us invariably that we have no way out, but to accept changes and undergo transformation!

CHAPTER FOUR

The Lesson Learnt

Sudha G

One day, while going to the final year class, I found a few boys sitting outside the classroom and chatting. I asked all of them to enter their respective classrooms. A few among them were from the final year class. I hadn't seen them in my class earlier. So, I asked them why they hadn't entered the classroom. The classes had begun almost 15 days earlier and they hadn't attended any of my classes. They apologised and said they will attend the classes regularly.

Allowing them to get into the class, I entered the class. After the students wished me, I asked them to sit and started marking the attendance. I didn't call the names of the long absentees at first. It was my habit to ask every student who had absented themselves in the previous class, his or her reason for not attending. After listening to their reasons, I would give them suggestions, and would ask them to attend classes regularly. I would tell them to inform me through their friends if they couldn't attend due to unavoidable circumstances. On those days, mobiles were not allowed in colleges.

Later I instructed them: "After watching you for one week, I will start marking the attendance and if you are regular, I will count your attendance from today." They all agreed and I began my lecture.

Next day, I noted all those who had attended the class. As one boy stood up and asked for the attendance, I repeated my condition stated earlier. He sat down and the class continued.

Next day, when I was about to enter the class, I saw that same boy sitting outside. I asked him "Why are you not attending the class?

He replied, "If you do not give me attendance, why should I attend? I will not attend."

Without pursuing him, I entered the classroom and started teaching my lesson. But my mind was disturbed over that boy's question. I was in a dilemma. I had no intention of punishing the boy by not giving attendance. I only wanted to bring some discipline in his life. Though I started revising the previous day's portion, my mind was restless.

I went out. He was lying down there on a bench. I called him and quite reluctantly, he got up. He carelessly asked me, "What now?"

Though I was angry and upset over his behaviour, I calmed myself & asked him, "If I give you attendance, will you attend my class?"

He replied immediately, "Yes."

I told him, " You shouldn't miss any class. Will you promise me?"

He thought for a while & said, "Definitely, except sometimes."

I said, "Sometimes, it is ok." He came along with me to class.

Once he entered the class & sat with his friends, I addressed the students, particularly keeping in mind the long list of absentees & said to them about my intentions of making them attend the classes regularly. "It is not just for attendance that you should attend classes but to learn about the subject. Moreover, this is the time you will learn many things which will mould your personality. I will try to make the lessons as interesting as possible. When you feel that my classes are boring, you can ask me to change my style of teaching or you can walk out of the class." Those boys listened to my words carefully, along with the other students.

Next day as I went to class, I saw all of them sitting in the class & some of them in the front benches. The particular boy was sitting on the third bench. My joy knew no bounds. But my responsibility had increased as I had told them that they could leave my class, if they felt it boring or if they felt they would not get anything new from the class. I had to take extra care to see that the classes were interesting. I used to teach them *National Power* fromthe *International Relations* paper. I used games like "Dog & Bone" to make them understand how countries fight for their interest and how power becomes very important. All got interested. The boys were actively involved in the game. As the bell was about to go I was curious to know their impression about that day's class. After the bell, when I was leaving the class, a few boys, particularly this boy, came to me and told, "Miss, we feel sorry that we did not attend your classes all these days. It was quite interesting and we will come regularly."

I had my first victory. But I was yet to see whether this very interest in them continues till the next day. Next day, again I saw all of them sitting and this boy had moved from the third bench to the second bench which was to remain his permanent bench throughout the year.

During that entire semester and the next one, I never saw him missing classes except for a few and every time when he wanted to leave, he sought my permission.

He listened very attentively along with his friends, responded to questions, raised questions sometimes, asked doubts, participated in all our department activities.

When he left the college, on the final day, he said to me, "Miss, because I did not want to miss your class, many times after jogging and sports in the morning, I used to go home, get ready and come without eating anything. But you gave us some snacks every day and it helped me a lot. (I used to provide some snacks to students everyday as they would come very early to college travelling by bus for more than half an hour or one hour. Sometimes they would walk 2-3 kilometers before catching the bus. Many students could not afford to bring lunch boxes). Even if you hadn't given me, I would have gone home and come back without eating. But thank you, Ma'am, for making me realise my worth. You always encouraged me in my passion to fare well in sports but asked me to complete my Undergraduate studies. I have cleared all papers during the last semester, and this semester too, I will do well in all the subjects. I haven't seen any such teacher at the college level coming to students and convincing them to attend classes. Thanks for everything."

I felt overwhelmed. I thanked him, telling: "You showed to me that our little care & concern can do wonders. I never thought I could make you attend classes regularly. It was just a try."

"It was your concern that changed me. Subjects, maybe I could have studied myself and passed. But I would have missed all other things that I learnt, which I feel will be very helpful in my future life. Once again Thank you very much."

His smile brightened up my face and my decision to strive to become a better teacher got strengthened because this incident showed me that "We can touch lives, Change lives." And that is for what we are hired for.

From 'Doctor's Set' to Teacher's Desk: An Unexpected Journey in Education

Achamma Alex

I was born on Teachers' *Day*!!! When my parents gifted me a 'Doctor's Set' toy on my fifth birthday, my uncle who was a Medical Practitioner explained to me the use of various toy gadgets in it. Ever since then my wish was to become a doctor, as I was carried away by a false notion that only doctors could serve humanity. Teacher-student child-play was one of the favourite pastime activities of me and my cousins during our younger days but I never thought I would ever become a teacher. The very thought of standing before students with confidence and leading them to the academic world crammed with information, through lectures, that too, in an endearing way, always sent shivers down my spine! Even when I came across the dictum, "Teaching is the noblest of all professions," I could not accept it fully, because in my heart of hearts I had the craving to walk through the corridors of hospitals in a doctor's gown carrying a stethoscope in my hand. But quite unexpectedly, I became a teacher!

Chemistry was my major subject for Undergraduate programme, but I had very little flair for Mathematics, which was my minor course. The low marks scored for Mathematics, was a hurdle in front of me to pursue my studies in Chemistry. I had scored very good marks for Part I English, and so, my parents and cousins encouraged me to choose English as my major subject for post-graduation. During my younger days, at least in Assumption College, Changanacherry, where I did my Pre-degree and Degree studies (1979- '84), girls who opted for English and Home Science were from families of planters. Their parents wanted to get them married off at a young age, preferably after graduation. I never wanted to get married young, and moreover, my parents had a comparatively broader outlook and always encouraged me to get employed. However, half-heartedly, I chose English Language and Literature for my higher studies.

I joined St. Berchmanns' College, Changanacherry, in 1984. One of my professors, who was also a priest, was well aware of my wish to pursue higher studies in Chemistry. One day while addressing the whole class he told us that there may be instances when we are forced to marry a boy or a girl against our conviction, but once we get married it is our duty to love the person whole-heartedly. Professor was indirectly telling me that I should learn to love the English Language and Literature. I got immersed in it as I delved deeper to unearth the hidden beauties of English Literature, and now I believe that it was the best choice I could have taken. Those two years shaped me into a good human being. My teachers at Berchmanns' taught me the need to read deeply prior to my classes and how to be sincere in teaching and guiding students. On completion of the Programme I was placed at Mar Thoma College for Women, Perumbavoor, on a temporary vacancy. There was a great demand for English teachers at that time. Many of my friends who had majored in Science subjects were running around frantically searching for job opportunities.

My first day at Perumbavoor college was quite memorable! As I stepped into a class of 90 girl students demurely, the class got hushed up. After marking the attendance, I introduced myself. As I introduced myself, I took notice of a girl sitting at the extreme right of the front row. She was staring at my face with wonder! Students introduced themselves one by one, and when her turn came, I asked her why she was gazing at me with wonder? Her answer made everyone in the class laugh. After the faculty interview, the Principal of the college had exhibited the list of selected candidates on the College notice board. Students who saw the name "Achamma Alex", expected a grey haired, middle aged woman with spectacles, holding an umbrella as their new teacher. When I stepped into the class (I was 23 years old at that time) they were wonderstruck.

This student holds a special place in my teaching career. She was very close to me and reminded me of my duty to my teachers. Her parents shared their daughter's appreciation of me as her teacher. Their words of appreciation in fact motivated me to become a better teacher. As the vacancy at Perumbavoor expired, in 1988 I got appointed at Christian College, Chengannur, affiliated to the University of Kerala. Subsequent to my marriage, I settled at Tiruvalla. It is quite surprising that she later became a teacher in a Higher Secondary school near my home town and got married to an alumnus of the college where I worked, and settled near my college. Years later, I could even teach her eldest son! She visited me invariably on all "Teachers' Day" with tokens of her love. She reminded me of the famous Chinese saying: **"A teacher a day is a father for a lifetime,"** and proved beyond doubt that a caring, loving teacher will be loved in turn by her students. I would undoubtedly say that the feedback of my students and teachers have assuredly contributed to my development as a teacher.

During the early days of my career at Christian College, where I continued till my retirement, I used to go to classrooms with lessons apportioned for each day. Once while teaching in a Pre-degree class, when the topic set aside for that particular day was over, I found there were 15 more minutes remaining for the final bell to go.

Being the last hour of a day, the students were restless and they were in a mood to go home. So, I decided to wind up the class and let the students off. They left the class with an uproar causing disturbance to neighbouring classes and shocking the Principal. As soon as I reached my Department staff room, I was called back by the Principal. When I reached the class, I saw that he had already ordered the students to get back to class. He accused me of dereliction of duty and chided me for winding up the class before the scheduled time. The students were sorry to witness my sad plight and promised me never to cause any trouble in the class again. They kept their word, and during the rest of the year they presented themselves as a batch of loving, caring and disciplined students. I am grateful to the students and Principal for necessitating the need to mend my class handling tactics, which stood in good stead in my future teaching career!

In my new college I was the junior most in a Department of 13 teachers. My senior faculty members were friendly and they all surprised me by their erudition. During free-time, I enjoyed listening to their experiences, stories and comments on various local / national / international problems. Majority of the stories pertained to Prof. S. Kailasom the former Head of the Department, who had retired some months before my joining the institution. Prof. S. Kailasom was a mentor and father-figure to my senior friends in the Department. One of the stories that influenced me was his approach to students. One day one of the teachers brought 2 students to the Department who were caught playing cards during the class hour. The teacher presented them before Prof. Kailasom with the hope that he would reprimand them for their misconduct in class. Prof. Kailasom asked them about their parents, family, hobbies and appreciated their talent in playing cards. Before sending them back, he didn't forget to ask them to teach him how to play cards! All other teachers were literally stunned, but they never questioned their Professor. Next day, they were all shocked to see the two boys apologizing to Prof. Kailasom with deep remorse and promised him never to be careless in their studies again. The tail piece of this story was that the two boys later succeeded in their studies and career. The impact this incident had on me was immeasurable!

My Schooling was done at St. Anne's Girls High School, Chengannur, a convent school. My Head Mistress (of course, a nun) who was also my English teacher, conducted herself in the school in a modest and dignified way. She loved all her students, but was very strict in academic matters and discipline. Caning was the usual mode of punishment on those days as. What touched me the most was that while punishing children for violating school discipline, she hugged them to ensure that they will take the punishment in its true spirit and will mend their ways. Later in my life, as a teacher, Head of the Department and Principal, I followed this example set by my beloved teacher while dealing with issues of indiscipline among students.

All my teachers at Assumption College were friendly with students, but they used their inherent capabilities to churn students and bring their best to the top. They all came to college well-dressed, and we used to watch them stealthily to see how they decked themselves! While watching the awe-inspiring classes of my Professors who could continuously lecture for 1 hour keeping our level of interest at the pinnacle, I had ruled out the possibility of ever becoming a teacher! I admired their qualities, still I was not sure if I could lecture for 1 hour keeping up the interest of students!

At St. Berchmanns' College teachers respected PG students. The Professor & Head of the Department, who addressed us on the first day, reminded us that we all would become teachers in the near future, and teachers should learn to respect their students! It was a shocking piece of information for me! I could never think of teachers respecting students! He told us we need not stand up while wishing them *Good morning* and *Good Afternoon*! They taught me how I should deal with the students sitting in front of me.

Like most of you, my first teachers were my parents. My first classroom was our kitchen. The concept of home-schooling was not extant during those days. Every day by 9 a.m. I followed my mother to the kitchen carrying a steel box full of books, pencil, eraser, crayons. She taught me English & Malayalam alphabets, basic Arithmetic, music, dance and Colouring. It is my mother who told me that students are just like children to teachers, and students should listen to them like listening to their parents. She taught me *Matha, Pitha, Guru, Daivam.* Believe me, or not...My Kindergarten and Class 1 studies were completed under the efficient tutelage of my Mom, that too, in our kitchen! Later when my family relocated to Kerala, straight away I joined Class 2 after *an entrance test* to evaluate my level of knowledge!

As I grew up, my father reminded me of my duty to my homeland. I was born abroad, and could go back before completing 18 years of age. After my Pre-degree studies I insisted on going back. My father, whose mind always brimmed with love for his motherland explained to me why I should give up the idea of going back. He was good in Maths and through calculations he proved to me that the fees I paid at Assumption College was not commensurate with the salary paid to my teachers by the Government. I was confused listening to him. He elucidated his economic theory and made me realise that the people of Kerala, even the poorest of the poor, were paying for my education through their direct and indirect taxes (There was no GST at that time!). I sensed my father's wish and gave up the idea of going abroad. Even at that point of time I never thought I would become a teacher! He always told me that an expatriate, even if he procures citizenship in a foreign land, will never be deemed as an equal citizen by the natives of the country. For him, a person needed self -esteem the most, and it could be realized only in one's own land!

Once, in Christian College, we had an M.A. batch with only 4 students — 2 girls and 2 boys. Three of them are now teachers. The husband of one of them told me that whenever his wife (of course, my student!) faced a problem in her life, she used to tell him that I had already predicted such possible crises in life. One day, while he got annoyed, he asked her, "Is there anything your Sudha Miss hasn't taught you?" I consider his comment as a positive accolade. When I joined Rajagiri, their eldest daughter was in her Final Year UG class. I have students who are clerical assistants, teachers, priests, bank employees, journalists, writers, movie directors, and those who have won Panorama Literature Festival Special Jury Award, Global Youth Icon award and the like. When my teacher-students tell me how they try to copy my example in their teaching career, I feel content. They all make it a point to text me messages once in a year because (I hope you remember, eh?) my birthday falls on "Teachers' day"!

I even remember an instance when I was travelling by train from Trivandrum to Tiruvalla, along with a Psychiatrist practicing at Mavelikkara. He told me how he used to direct some of his mentally unsettled young patients to our Department because he was sure they would be well taken care of. For me, the confidence the Doctor had in me and my colleagues was just like receiving the Oscar Nomination! I especially remember two of my brilliant students who were constantly under psychiatric care. They were tense during their exams. Me and my colleagues used to sit by their side encouraging and pacifying them. Both of them are now teachers, and they give me surprise calls once in a while!

It would be a grievous offense if I fail in acknowledging the role played by Dr. Jameela Begum, my M.Phil and Ph.D. supervising teacher at the Institute of English, who had been a "friend, philosopher and Guide" to me since 1994. During moments of inner turmoil and confusion, she was all ears, patiently listening to my agonies, to help me find solutions to my problems. I have certainly imbibed that quality from her which I tried to put into practice while dealing with students who came to me with troubled minds.

My teachers at the school and college levels have also shown me the importance of merging curricular with co-curricular programmes to keep up the agility and energy levels of students while they are on campus. I think I have assimilated all these lessons. I have tried to practise them wisely and judiciously. By the grace of God Almighty, I could put in 34 years of teaching service in the aided sector wherein I served as a Lecturer, Senior Grade

Lecturer, Selection Grade Lecturer, Associate Professor, Head of the Post Graduate Department, and eventually I retired as the Principal of the institution. I retired on 31 March 2000, during the 'lockdown' period of Covid-'19 Pandemic. During the next two years the world had come to a standstill. When all teachers who were in active service busied themselves with online teaching, I too became an online teacher for the PG students of Bishop Kurialacherry College, Amalagiri, and Theology students of Hebron Theological Seminary, Kumbanad. As everything got back to normal, I became restless at the thought that I could no longer address students in a classroom. God answered my prayers and led me to Rajagiri College of Social Sciences (Autonomous) where I teach, presently.

All these years I have tried to become an understanding, compassionate, selfless, responsible, duty-bound, self-esteemed, patient teacher, respecting the students sitting in front of me and loving them as my own children. I tried to mould them into socially sensitive and responsible 'human beings.' My elder daughter was also my student for her UG and PG studies. I was so happy to get her enrolled there because I was confident of the type of education and training we provided to students at Christian College.I bettered my academic qualifications with an M.Phil and Ph. D. degrees and tried to disseminate the little knowledge and expertise I had procured through my higher studies. I invariably spend my classes to teach my children what life is, how to face problems in life, the need to become empathetic, and their duty to serve their motherland. My examples were mostly from my family and my own life. There were moments when my elder daughter got embarrassed when I exemplified situations in lessons with domestic illustrations. At one point of time she even warned her younger sister (who was 8 years younger to her!) to be careful about what they did at home! If any of my students remember me today, I am sure, they will remember me for the guidance I have given them as to how to face challenges in life. I am grateful to my parents, teachers, colleagues and students who have played vital roles in transforming me to a real teacher.

In the Post-Covid scenario, when discussions are going on to minimise classroom teaching and substitute teachers with robots and AI, I feel it is high time we sense the need of putting our children under the care and guidance of good teachers *who practice good values rather than teach*, to shape them into good human beings. India is perhaps the first country in the world to practice a residential system of education. Our forefathers used to put their children in *Gurukuls* under a *Guru*. The children received holistic education that nurtured them physically, intellectually, emotionally and spiritually. Many people and youngsters may consider this as unnecessary and out of date procedure. We create intellectuals, but they cease to become human beings. EQ is as important as IQ. This is what our children need today.

As I move down the memory lane, I feel I have made the right choice in my life. If I had landed up in some other profession, I would have quit earlier. I always remind myself that being a teacher, I should be a ladder enabling my children to scale greater heights of success! While trying to better my own academic brilliance, I should never be a mercenary leaving my children to wander in the mire and get lost. Let us go for an educational system that provides holistic education to our future generations, shaping them into good human beings, intellectually bright and useful citizens!

CHAPTER SIX

My Teaching Experience

Marie Pierre Augustin

Though I sincerely feel that I have not achieved great things in my career, I deem it a great pleasure to share my humble teaching experience.

To say the truth, at the beginning of my career I wished to become a doctor. That was also the wish of my parents. Hence, I chose the science group in my Pre-University. Though I could not enter a medical college, I still continued with Zoology in my Undergraduate studies. It was during my days as a UG student in Loyola college, that Lord made me realise my vocation as a teacher. In my class I had a lot of friends who had done their schooling in Tamil medium. Since the medium of instruction was English, they found it very difficult. So, I took it upon myself to conduct group study and explain our lessons to them in simple English. It was then that I realised that my vocation was not to become a doctor but to become a Teacher. The special coaching classes I offered to my friends truly inspired and motivated me to become a Teacher.

Soon after my Post Graduation and M.Phil studies in French, I started my career as Assistant Professor of French in PSG college of Arts and Science, Coimbatore, in July 1979.

For one year I taught French as part I language to our UG students. In October 1980, by God's grace I was awarded with a one-year French Government scholarship to undergo a training course (DPFE) to teach French as a foreign language at CLA, Besançon, (Centre de de linguistique appliqué France). On my return from France in December 1981, I joined the Department of French of Madurai Kamaraj University as lecturer. Apart from teaching the PG and M.Phil students, I had to handle classes for students of Certificate / Diploma and Higher Diploma courses. These were Beginners' courses conducted during the evenings for employed professionals.

Being a teacher at the university level, I had to pursue my research and do my PhD. I successfully completed my doctorate in French under the very able guidance of my Guru and Professor (Dr) Rajeswari Chandrasekhar in 1995. The topic chosen was "Translation, Commentary and Structural Analysis of Tamil short stories: Paramartha Gourouvin Kathai." On completion of my Doctoral studies, I was promoted as Associate Professor in 1995 and later as Professor in 2003. In 1997, by Divine Providence, I had the golden opportunity of getting the French government scholarship to undergo a specialisation course for 2 years in Translation at the world-renowned institute ISIT in Paris. My special thanks are due to our Department Professor and Head, Dr. Rajeswary who encouraged me and helped me in procuring a special study leave for 2 years from our university. This course enabled me to become an expert in translation. I translated some of our renowned Tamil literature works such as *Naladiyaar Poems* into French. This project was given to me by CICT (Central Institute of Classical Tamil). This also helped me to guide our research scholars to undertake research works in Translation. Along with my duty as a teacher, from 2003 onwards, I even shouldered the responsibility of being the Head of the Department.

During my tenure as the Head of the Department, many seminars and conferences, both at The national and international levels, were organised. Under my guidance 9 research scholars completed their Doctoral studies. I also had the opportunity to visit Canada for one month under Shastri-Indo Canadian Institute. I also started many new courses, such as certificate and diploma courses through distance education. After 33 years of long service in our Department, I took my retirement in June 2015. However, again through Divine Providence, the University Grants Commission, nominated me as Emeritus Professor for 2 years with the project of translating Gabrielle Roy's Novel- *Rue Duchambault* into Tamil. I completed the project successfully in 2017 and retired from the active teaching profession in June 2017. Though I have retired from active life, I still continue to help our students to prepare for their Net exams along with my Professor Mme Rajeswari. I also help research scholars who are doing their PhD.

When I took up the profession as a French teacher in PSG college I did not face much challenge since French was just taught as Part I language. After my training in France, when I joined our Department, I had to face a great challenge. At the Postgraduate Level, French had to be taught in depth as a major subject with literature, linguistics etc. Majority of Students who joined the course had only a knowledge of the French Language at the basic level. Hence, many of the students who joined, got discouraged as they were unable to follow the course. We had to take the challenge of encouraging these students to continue the course by giving them special coaching classes during their first semester. This bridge course went a long way to help those students to overcome their problems and come out successful with a Master's Degree in French after 2 years. During these years of teaching and research, students' welfare and development was my main concern. Along with my colleagues I extended my support to students without any discrimination of creed, caste or social status. Making money was not our top priority. Gradually these core values provided me with job satisfaction and achievements in my career. I was certainly privileged to work in that second home amidst students from various backgrounds. Today they are in various corners of the world practicing this amazing language: FRENCH

Though I feel I have done my best as a teacher, I am not still satisfied, since I feel that I could have still done better. I still have a passion towards the teaching profession and I shall continue till my health permits. I wish to thank Rajagiri College of Social Sciences, Kalamassery, Cochin, for having given me this opportunity to share my Teaching Experience. Let me express my sincere heartfelt gratitude to our Lord who was the pioneer in moulding me as a teacher. I owe all my success as a teacher to Him. It was He who was behind every stage of my career.

CHAPTER SEVEN

Learning / Teaching: In the Classroom and Beyond

Sheila Elizabeth Abraham

It has always been my wish to become a teacher, as far as my memory goes. In fact, we have a long tradition of teachers in my family. Both my parents, as well as my maternal grandfather were teachers; long before that, my maternal grandmother's father also happened to be a teacher. I suppose that is how the idea of teaching as the noblest profession got instilled into my consciousness.

Every teacher once was a student, so naturally, my reminiscences as a teacher are a continuum of my student days. It is an accepted fact that for a child, parents are the first teachers, and teachers are the second parents. However, the children of teachers used to perform so well in studies, especially in our childhood, when university education was not yet common.

Ours was a small family having only two daughters, a rarity for the times. My elder sister managed to secure admission for MBBS after her B.Sc., and the same thing must have been expected of me as well. Nevertheless, having missed the admission to MBBS by a few marks, I decided to pursue English Language and Literature for my Degree Programme.

Those three years gave me the opportunity for a lot of extra-curricular activities as well as wide reading. Having grown up almost like an only child, as my sister was quite senior to me, and mostly living in the hostel, I developed a penchant for reading early in life. It became my favorite pastime, also because there weren't many diversions other than the radio and occasional films.

I studied at Mar Thoma College, Tiruvalla, for five years, where the foundations were laid for the study of English Language and Literature. The words of William Wordsworth rang true for us:

"Bliss was in that dawn to be alive

But to be young was very heaven"

But the real edifice was built at St. Berchmanns' College, Changanacherry, where I did my Masters. The college boasted a rich tradition. The wit and wisdom of Prof. C.A. Sheppard was proverbial, though he had long since left the institution. He was a great Shakespeare scholar and had founded the Berchmanns' Theatre, mainly for staging the Great Bard's plays.

I was astounded by the profundity of scholarship and extreme dedication of the teachers. Some of them seemed hardly aware of the bell announcing the end of the hour or day. Their meticulous handling of the portions influenced me so much that I emulated their example in my teaching, reading all the critical works available and never skipping any part of the syllabus. It is possible that some of my students found such exhaustive treatment a bit exhausting! But that is my tribute to the great Professors of St. Berchmanns'. Special mention has to be made of Prof. V.J. Augustine, the Head of the Department, and Prof. A.E. Augustine, another scholarly figure.

Though we passed with high hopes of lecturing away at full swing in some college, the academic scenario was rather disconcerting, as very few vacancies arose in those lean years. Then the Government of Kerala decided to introduce the Shift system in colleges in order to accommodate the disproportionate number of students who became eligible for college education as a result of the liberalized policy.

That was how I joined the Department of English, Mar Thoma College, Tiruvalla, in 1980. By a stroke of luck, my date of appointment coincided with Teachers day, that is, 5 September. I joined a 25-strong Department which had housed many stalwart figures. Two of the Vice Chancellors of the University of Kerala had started their career there—Dr. A.V. Varghese and Dr. J.V. Vilanilam. Dr. Varghese, in fact, had been the architect of the Post Graduate Department. I gratefully remember Prof. C.C. Joseph, Prof. C.T. Titus, Prof. Leelamma Joseph and Prof. Babu Zachariah who have influenced me in different but unique ways.

To be honest, it was a bit unnerving to be seated with one's own Professors. Neverthless, they exuded good will and affection for me as, I may presume, a favourite student. It was customary to arrange an annual family picnic which brought everyone closer, in course of time. When five more lecturers joined next year, we felt sort of "seniorish". Well, years passed, there were retirements, and new faces appeared. Finally, it was time for me to retire in 2009.

As Head of the Department, I endeavoured to be fair and impartial to everyone. In turn, I received the support of my colleagues and students in a great measure. During my tenure, we conducted two National seminars successfully. The first time it was really tough as we had little experience and hardly any capital. But we managed well by putting in generous contributions from our side.

I had diverse experiences with my colleagues in my career spanning about three decades. Initially, I had a score of my own teachers in the Department whom I treated with deference. There was camaraderie more with those who joined along with me or soon after. During the last phase of my career, I had some of my own students as my junior colleagues. Incidentally, I have had the good fortune to teach the children of my early batch of students.

Many of my students have scaled heights in different walks of life. Blessey, the distinguished film director, was my student during my first year. Nayantara (then Diana) joined our Department for the Degree programme in English, which she could not complete, as she was very soon absorbed on to the silver screen. Actor Prashanth Alexander, Actor / Director Siddharth Sivaprasad, Chef Naushad and Jovitta Thomas who works with the UNO, are some of our well known alumni. I narrowly missed teaching Adv. Mathew T.Thomas, MLA of Tiruvalla, as he was in the senior B.Sc. class.

There were many opportunities to interact with students outside the classroom. As Director of the Brains Trust, of which I had been a member in my student days, I conducted regular meetings and annual camps. The Golden Jubilee of the Brains Trust was celebrated in a memorable manner. We also had regular Tutorial hours with about a dozen students under each mentor for individual care.

I have also accompanied the students on tour on several occasions. One was to Kanyakumari and en route we visited Shri Padmanabha palace where quite by chance we had the good luck to meet Mohanlal during the shooting of *"His Highness Abdulla"*. Another trip was to Wynad which we all enjoyed, and the present devastation of the place is heartbreaking.

My career was also one of professional growth. When I joined service, I was all too confident about my eligibility to lecture to PG students. It was nothing short of an anticlimax to find that junior lecturers were considered good only for junior classes. It took about five years for me to step into a PG class. There followed a period of intense study and preparation.

When the first opportunity presented itself for the Faculty Improvement Programme, I happily applied. Once you got selected, the next step was to secure admission for M.Phil. We had been part of the University of Kerala till 1983, when Mahatma Gandhi University was established. As a university in its infancy, MG University had no M.Phil. programmes yet. So, some of us prepared a memorandum and presented it to Dr. U.R. Anantamurthy, the then Vice-Chancellor, when he came to the college to deliver the Dr. A.V. Varghese Memorial Lecture. As the first signatory, I along with others, tried to convince him of our unhappy predicament. However, a solution was arrived at when the University of Kerala took a decision to increase the number of Teacher Fellows from 3 to 6. When I joined the Institute of English, Trivandrum, in 1988, it seemed a sort of poetic justice as I had earnestly desired to do my

Masters there.

It was at the Institute of English that I came across the atmosphere of research culture. However, my exhilaration could not be sustained. As the mother of two kids below the age of ten, staying at the YWCA, Trivandrum, coming home every Friday and leaving by an early train on Monday, my life was rendered acutely hectic. The saddest memory of those days is about my father meeting with an accident hardly three weeks into my course, causing him to be bedridden for four months till his death.

Neverthless, my stay in Trivandrum for a full year was instrumental in broadening my horizons. The invigorating presence of Dr. Ayyappa Panikkar, the Head of the Institute, transformed us in several ways. Visiting The British Library, Kerala University Library, and Calicut University Library helped a lot in the days when the internet was not freely available. These experiences later motivated me to visit many famous universities the world over.

I got another chance for Faculty Improvement while completing my Ph. D. from Mahatma Gandhi University. Visiting the American Studies Research Centre in Hyderabad, with its centralized A/c library and adjacent hostel, was a boon to research scholars. Going to the Central Institute of English and Foreign Languages was a bonus. I made several further trips to ASRC for a Summer Fellowship and a Refresher Course in American Literature.

I liked to attend Refresher courses even before they were mandatory. I attended one in Mahatma Gandhi University and another in Kerala University, as well as a workshop on Canadian Literature at the Institute of English.

Another event that fostered fellowship with teachers from the same discipline was the centralized valuation camp. It was also a venue for exchanging views and news. Valuing the answer sheets gave glimpses of some humorous anecdotes. Once a Pre-degree student attempted an essay on the problem of Beggars. The solution suggested by this student was to take all beggars of the city in a ship and sink the ship in the mid ocean!

Being a member of the PG Board of Exams and conducting viva-voce for M.A. students became a routine duty towards the end of my career.

Passing through different designations, from Junior Lecturer to Lecturer, Later Lecturer Senior Scale to Lecturer Selection Grade, and finally to Associate Professor, I retired at the age of 55. However, it seemed to descend on me all too soon when I had enough time to devote to my career, being relatively free from familial duties. So, I accepted the offer for a part time faculty position of PG course at Bishop Kurialacherry College, Amalagiri. It was a fruitful and satisfying tenure for me as I enjoyed the ambience of a well-run women's college with the affection of the students and the cordial nature of the faculty. I have always cherished my association with Dr. Rekha Mathews. The college has a well-stocked library that I made good use of. I had brief spells of teaching in some other institutions as well. I could also procure a Post-Graduate Diploma in Counselling after retirement.

From my observations I have noticed one weakness in teachers, that is, to spot mistakes in speech and writing. This particularly applies to language teachers like me. Once a teacher, always a teacher!

After my formal retirement, I got plenty of opportunities for travelling. While in service, I had undertaken only one international travel. But my husband and I started travelling in earnest subsequent to our retirements. We have visited almost all the Indian states and about 30 countries. As Francis Bacon observes, "Travel in the younger sort is a part of education, in the elder, a part of experience." Visiting a place, you have read about makes it more meaningful. Conversely, speaking of relevant travel experiences while teaching makes it more enjoyable. My visit to London, Globe Theatre and Stratford-upon-Avon was a dream come true.

So finally, when all is said and done, retirement is not a bad situation because retirement opens the door to freedom — to teach, read, write, travel, serve society, or be perfectly at ease. I have chosen an active life, serving the various bodies of the Mar Thoma Church, including Women's Fellowship.

During my teaching career spanning 44 years, I have had the good fortune to teach tens of thousands of students. It is quite heart-warming to come across an old student every now and then, even in far off places like the USA. Like grown up children developing to the best friends of parents, there are at least a few students who have become my trusted friends. A few years ago, the Higher Secondary teachers of Syrian Christian Seminary School, Tiruvalla, decided to celebrate Teachers Day by honouring their own teachers from each Department. My loving student Anu Philip invited me and I took a class for her students. The memory is all the dearer to me as she is no more.

I have heard it said that teaching is just like making a long-term deposit. You start getting the dividends much later in life in the form of acknowledgement, appreciation, affection, and care from your students. In that respect, I can certainly affirm that the investment I have made in my students has brought in ample dividends, and continues to do so even after all these years.

CHAPTER EIGHT

Story of Student- Teacher Relationship

Shaleen Kumar Singh

In 2020, on November 21st, Dr. Gyanendra Maheshwari turned sixty-five, burdened by an almost premonitory fear—his Guru had passed away at sixty-four. The bond between them was so profound and mystical that he believed he wouldn't outlive the age his Guru had reached. Their connection began in the early seventies when Dr. Maheshwari first met Dr. Vinai Kumar Singh. From that moment, there was no looking back. He often recounted the same stories of my father to me, and we never tired of them, recognizing that they conveyed timeless wisdom.

He vividly recalls the first time he saw my father and how captivated he was by his presence. "Guddu, papaji ki angrezi badi tabadtod hoti thi tab..." (Back then, your father's command of English was remarkable), he tells me. As their relationship deepened, he would often say, "Guruji ne to jeevan ki disha hi badal di" (Guruji completely changed the course of my life).He learnt about Osho, Satya Sai Baba, Paramahns Yogananda, Meher Baba, Swami Ram, Ramakrisha Paramhans, Lobsang Rampa and so many other sufi saints from my father... He also learnt how to write poetry...And what he learnt about poetry was that it can not be written...Actullly poetry writes the poet...

From then on he was a shadow of my father...After the lethal scooter accident of my father, he proved to be the best aide. When the chilly cold winter was on its peak, my father used to go in the wee hours to join college. Father's disciple was always standing and waiting for his guru Ji so that his guru Ji may reach safely to his room and from making tea to every household support he provided to his guru. He was doing every work that we had to do or my mother had to do to assist my father.

I still marvel now as to what force of love and gratitude he had been filled with that he kept on serving his guru for all these years. His love kept on flowing incessantly for long so many years to his Guru and after his guru's demise to his family i.e. mother, brother, and I. What treasure did my father give him, that he kept on showering his love, care, and blessing to us all.

That was something so great that I can't measure...probably no one ...

He has grown into someone very insecure, unfortunate, depressed, yet full of love towards God. He instilled nearly all merits of the father. He had imbibed nearly all truths that father whispered in his ears sometime in his long conversations that he fortunately had daily in Dibai.

Today he called me and said, "*Chhote, Mai tumse naraz hun, tumne mujhe birthday wish nahi kiya...*" I said, "*Bhai Sahab, Galati go gayi...bhool gya...*" he said, "*chalo koi bat nahi..*"

His name is Dr. Gyanendra Maheshwari. He is a Ph.D. on the poetry of Bhavani Prasad Mishra. He is a prolific poet with many collections to his credit. He has been as ill-fated as my father ie his guru. Once my father wrote about him while writing the preface of his thesis as his **quondam** student. Fathermay call him a former student as he was sometimes a student of his class. When at an age of sixty-five, I look at him, I find him still as disciplined into *guru shishya parampara*.

I too am a teacher; I know that there are always some students who always encroach the terrain of class and be your family members. Dr. Gyanendra is one of those chosen few. He is always with us...Like our eldest brother...Like the replica of father...Like the one who reminds us the fact that teachers are not just human entity, teachers are immortal traditions......Like the one who reminds that not everything that you sow in the desert will perish.... there are always certain possibilities of light in dark.

At 65 now Dr. Gyanendra says what Bernie Taupin wrote in a song of Elton John, "I've no wish to be living sixty years on" Even in telephonic conversations with he says, "Guru ji left us at 64...." He said, "*Main kaise itne din zinda rah gya...*"

Probably no disciple wishes to live more than his/her teacher. Long or short, a disciple is always brimmed with respect and adoration to his/her teacher. He/she wishes to be as relevant, useful and as his/her teacher.

Dr Gyanendra establishes that teacher leave indelible footprints on the sands on time.

Here is his pic. He rarely allowed me to click him.

Putting on Bata sandak (He even started putting on this after he saw his guru in this.)

CHAPTER NINE

Forging the Creative Space

Seema Bhaduri

Creativity, an element of the divine, brings out the best in woman (man included). One is generally most productive and happy in the environment that inspires one's talents to flourish. A liberal atmosphere is most likely to spur the creative instinct. As a lecturer - professor in language and literature studies for thirty plus years, I saw a large number of students including the usually dull, passive and distracted ones, metamorphosing into circuits of creative engagement with class-room and outdoor activities and at the same time, evolving into brighter performers.

It has generally been observed that while not much can be taught per se within class-room time, a great deal of learning does happen if the same class becomes a happening place. Text-books when seen and used in class not as ends in themselves but as windows to the real-life world, do inspire a lot of lateral learning. The art as many of us know, lies in transforming textual matter into experiential awareness. By comparing the given textual matter with what transpires by the day closer home, by prodding students to draw parallels between the two, by initiating relevant dialogue, young minds can indeed be spurred on to unraveling the text in multiple ways. With such exercises the atmosphere in class brightens up, the enjoyment quotient increases. Where, as it often happens in compulsory language classes that the course-work isn't very engaging at least to the more intelligent students, a teacher can introduce add-on reading activities based on abridged classics and informative journals, bring in varied and interactive exercises in language learning and communication skills, call for book-reviews, wall-paper and essay writings, and so on. My personal experience has shown that while not all students can be persuaded to join in, those that do attain a greater proficiency in their overall performance. Even today the committed teacher remains the student's best and final link to the entire teaching program. She is that catalyst who moulds the syllabus into an ever fresh and invigorating source of multi-dimensional learning.

Where literature learning is concerned the teacher's emphasis could well be on presenting the content with a comparative perspective, juxtaposing the given matter with similar scenes, situations and characters drawn from other texts or cultures, or media. This would induce students to look at texts from various angles. Questions such as why the ending in D.H.Lawrence's *Sons and Lovers* wouldn't commonly apply to Indian society, why a Lady Wishfort of *The Way of the World* would be a misfit in the Indian social context, or why unlike T.S. Eliot's waste-landers Indians do not look on April as the cruellest month, could indeed help students play with meanings, get beneath the skin of the text.

In our classrooms we sought also to cross-connect the various literary pieces being taught in different classes to bring alive their mutual inter-relations in order to evoke for students some of the common streams of thought in literature. This exercise helped stimulate their attention towards their texts.

With us, the floor of even the regular PG classroom often doubled up as the site for debate and discussion, group presentations, pair-work, silent reading exercises, note-making together of-course with the intermittent question-answer sessions. This kept the students hooked and alert. Bringing text-book, note-book and dictionaries to class was mandatory. Each one knew that she was being closely monitored. While taking down notes she was aware of the teacher walking up and down the aisle, peering into her notebook to spot possible errors in spelling, to make sure her writing was legible. Result, even those who joined from other colleges and occasionally, from the science and commerce streams as well, soon realized they would have to perform. They saw that while we were downright stringent with grades and marks we were equally lavish with our inputs in teaching, that their performance mattered to us.

Weekly library visits were obligatory, these being often cross-checked with the Librarian himself. We insisted as well that students stay back on the campus after the classes, eat their tiffins together and do their homework collectively and whenever necessary, consult us as well. This measure yielded fruit. The weaker students who came in large numbers from rural areas soon became part of larger groups, interacting mutually. Where the bonding is emotionally rich, the output is bound to be better. While some of our students became University rank-holders, a handsome percentage of the rest soon found place as lecturers in the colleges around.

Our Department had the immense advantage of having a Language Lab meant for classes in Functional English, an optional course at the undergrad level. This was a hall of around 450 sq feet equipped with language booths, a TV, an overhead projector, gramophone records, tapes and videos, and books on language learning. This rich assembly of gadgets had however been kept securely under lock and key all along, to be put on display exclusively for important visitors. Securing a nod from the higher authorities, I had this lab opened up for our numerous activities. The gadgets now became the students' property. A weekly Open Class program of an hour's duration was initiated. Any student of the Department could simply walk in during this period and watch educational as well as classical programs, play the tapes and videos, debate and discuss with others, rehearse plays, or else, simply read the books that we had transferred from our homes to our recently instituted departmental library.

Our Lab therefore buzzed with activity. After regular classes were done, the monthly programs of our newly constituted Dramatics Club, Cinema Club and Literary Association took the space over, turn by turn. Students from other departments too joined in off and on; there were no restrictions. The Department had become a lively, creative hub and the college was proud of this. We had more students of calibre joining us. Plays from Shakespeare and Chekhov, William Goldsmith and Girish Karnad came to be staged.

The increasing quality of performance and the growing popularity of these activities led us to starting the annual English Litt - Fest. It was generally a two-day program with essay-writing and elocution competitions scheduled for day one. The next day was given to for on-stage activities. Our students performed on make-shift stages raised by themselves underneath the green canopies of those ancient trees that our campus is famous for. Remarkable here is the fact that these young minds planned, organized and conducted the entire set of programs themselves of course with some guidance from us. Even the rehearsals were largely their own doing; we dropped in but occasionally to explain the text and direct the performance. Drama, dance, mime and song all were allowed. Students across the spectrum – from the convent educated to those from the vernacular mediums including the brilliant and otherwise – all joined in. The plays drew the maximum following.

It was heartening to see students with little knowledge of spoken English otherwise, performing with confidence and flair. The high point of creativity however arrived when a couple of years later, the brighter students began writing and directing their own plays at the Fest. Their standards of performance were good. Their talent had taken wing.

These activities were a veritable mine of learning as well, for they blended entertainment with increasing involvement, exposing young minds to larger dimensions of awareness, ingraining in them the skills of group-work, discipline and accountability. We took pains to ensure maximum participation, roping in students for off-stage activities such as the make-up, the stage-construction, the audience-management and the anchoring. We had thus enabled many indifferent students to become motivated performers. It was therefore a proud moment when our students staged their plays at the University for the first time in the history of our college. They also went on to bag the first prize for staging an adaptation of Arthur Miller's All my Sons at the American Road-show Competition. For us teachers however the greater happiness lay in watching the clear feel of satisfaction, the sense of belonging, of confidence and camaraderie which these boys and girls as a whole continued to exude throughout the span of their respective courses. This was an achievement and we felt proud!

Students as we all know so well, come loaded with a lot of mental baggage, with insecurities, repressed tensions, peer-pressures, domestic challenges and the like. There is evidence aplenty to show that this baggage affects their mental health and thereby, their performance. Having identified a couple of cases of physical molestation, and many more of depression, isolation, and fear psychosis in our classes our Department began a staggered weekly counselling program with each teacher sparing an hour per week after college work was done, to listen to and to counsel students. The allotment of teachers was made as per students' entries in the requisition chart that had been provided to them. It worked. Later on this chart became the blue-print for similar charts which other departments in our college were preparing on the eve of NAAC.

Admittedly we could do little here – we hadn't any training, nor even the required time. But we had definitely made a beginning. The students felt it and their acknowledgement was evident when many of them told us that this Department had virtually become their second home. We had arrived.

CHAPTER TEN

The Pappi Tales: Lessons from my Grandfather

Rincy Saji

In my early teaching career at Rajagiri College of Social Sciences, Kalamassery, I conducted a self-introduction exercise and asked my students what lessons they had learned in their twenties. Their answers were rich with personal experiences and insights. One student turned the question back to me: "Ma'am, what did you learn in your twenties?" This question stirred a reflection on the life lessons I've carried with me, lessons imparted by my grandfather, A.O. Pappachan, known affectionately as Pappi. In retrospect, I shared with them the invaluable lessons I learned from my grandfather, which I love to label as "The Pappi Tales." I explained how these tales are not just stories but cherished teachings that have guided me through life.

During the long summer vacations of my childhood in Kerala, we were wholly consumed by the enchanting world of books in my grandfather's library. My grandfather, A.O. Pappachan, is a man whose life was deeply intertwined with literature. His library at home was a testament to his love for books, featuring an eclectic mix ranging from Dostoevsky's profound psychological explorations to Hemingway's terse, yet emotionally charged prose. Shakespeare's dramatic genius, Ben Jonson's sharp wit, Tolstoy's sweeping epics, and J.K. Rowling's imaginative realms were all part of this literary mosaic. Additionally, the works of Basheer and M.T. Vasudevan Nair offered rich insights into Malayalam literature and culture. People often visited our home to borrow books, some even named it "The Pappi's Library."

In our small hometown, Grandpa was a revered figure known for his boundless generosity. Despite his own financial limitations, people often came to him seeking help, and he never turned them away. I distinctly remember asking him why he never asked for repayment for the money he lent out. With his usual warmth, he quoted Mother Teresa: "It is not how much we give, but how much love we put into giving." This poignant insight perfectly captured his philosophy of generosity.

This moment illuminated Grandpa's broader outlook on life. Much like his passion for literature, which he saw as a gateway to diverse worlds, he regarded generosity as a means to forge genuine connections and spread happiness. For Grandpa, the true value of giving was not in the material sum but in the love and compassion that each act embodied. His approach to generosity was a testament to his belief that the essence of a meaningful life lies in the heartfelt care we extend to others.

His lesson on learning also served as a guiding principle throughout my academic career, especially during my Ph.D. tenure. One day Pappi decided to take me to the Sri Adi Sankara Keerthi Sthamba Mandapam, Kalady, a towering monument honoring the great philosopher Adi Shankaracharya. As we reached the site, I was captivated by the monument's grandeur, enjoying the serene view it offered.rue to his nature, Pappi began lecturing me about the history of Adi Shankara, the significance of his teachings, and the importance of this very place. He went on and on, and after a while, I grew bored. "Pappi," I said, interrupting him, "can we just enjoy the view instead of another lecture?" Pappi gave me a gentle, knowing smile. "Where are you standing?" he asked. "This is the birthplace of Adi Shankara," I answered quickly. He nodded and followed with more questions: "Who was Adi Shankara? How tall is this monument? Who built it? Why do we celebrate it?" I realized I didn't have any answers.

Seeing my silence, Pappi softly said, "You see, knowledge is never complete. You can't ever know everything, but learning—learning is a journey that never ends. That's what matters." His words sank deep into my heart. That day, as I stood in front of the monument, I realized that Pappi wasn't just teaching me facts—he was teaching me that true education is about the pursuit of knowledge, not the illusion of knowing it all. It's a lesson that transformed the way I saw learning, not as a final goal but as a lifelong journey of discovery.

During my vacations in Kerala, I would often sit with Pappi on the veranda, narrating stories from school. One afternoon, I recounted an argument with a boy in my class who had stolen my pencil. Despite my attempts to confront him, he stubbornly refused to admit it. Frustrated, I asked Pappi why some people couldn't just admit when they were wrong. Pappi listened carefully, nodding as I spoke. When I finished, he leaned back and said, "You can wake someone who is sleeping, but you can never wake someone who is pretending to sleep." I looked at him, puzzled, and he explained further, "People who are not ready to understand or accept their mistakes are a waste of time to argue with. They've already made up their minds, and trying to make them see reason will only drain you."

He advised me to keep my distance from such people, for engaging in conversation with them wasn't just futile—it was mentally exhausting. "Save your energy for those who are willing to listen, learn, and grow," he said. This lesson stuck with me, and it became a guiding principle in my interactions with others. I realized that not every battle is worth fighting, and sometimes, the best course of action is to walk away. Pappi's wisdom taught me the importance of protecting my mental well-being and focusing my efforts on meaningful connections rather than draining arguments.

Pappi's library was not just a collection of books but a repository of life lessons. His ability to blend literary passion with practical wisdom was remarkable. He taught me that reading was not just an escape but a way to engage with the world more meaningfully. His insights on time management and lifelong learning have been invaluable in shaping my personal and professional life. One of the most impactful lessons Pappi taught me was about time. He believed that "There is no perfect time to do something." This philosophy was more than advice; it was a call to action. Pappi's perspective helped me realize that waiting for the "right" moment often means missing out on opportunities. His words encouraged me to seize the present and make the most of it, a lesson that has guided me through various phases of my life, including balancing a career, family responsibilities, and personal passions

As I shared these experiences with my students, I saw a range of reactions. Some understood and appreciated the essence of these lessons, while others merely heard them without fully grasping their depth. I realized that such lessons, though rich and profound, come with experience and time. They are like fresh buds—promising, but still in the process of blooming. In teaching, I aim to impart not just textbook knowledge but life lessons that resonate deeply and endure over time. As I often say, "The real value of education is seen in how its lessons continue to guide students long after graduation." These lessons from Pappi are like seeds planted in my students' minds. Some may grasp them immediately, while others will need time and experience to appreciate their value fully. Just as Pappi's wisdom continues to guide me, I hope to leave my students with lessons that will grow with them, enriching their lives as they navigate their own journeys.

CHAPTER ELEVEN

The Ripple Effect

Kavitha Gopalakrishnan

As I reflect on my 11 year teaching journey at the Department of English, Baselius College, Kottayam, I am reminded of the profound wisdom of Jacques Derrida: "I speak only one language, and it is not my own." I am thus making an attempt to pen words not my own but my students' with a sense of gratitude for the opportunity I got to touch their lives and shape their minds.

Teaching, for me, has never been just a profession; it's a calling, a responsibility, and a privilege that I cherish deeply. My attempt has forever been to cultivate inclusive, empathetic, and optimistic learning environments. My students have always acknowledged my efforts to create a safe space where every individual feels valued, heard, and respected.

In a class scenario, we get to meet different kinds of students, and the stance I take with each of them is reminiscent of what Ulysses says about Telemachus in Tennyson's poem: "He works his work, I mine." This approach has not gone unnoticed. One of my students once told me that the respect I give to my students is something he loves, as I show no favoritism and I'm not pushy. Yet, at the same time, I keep reminding them that they should strive to be the best of their ability.

Optimism is a cornerstone of my approach. I believe in empowering students to transform challenges into opportunities, to find the silver lining in every circumstance. This mindset enables them to navigate life's complexities with resilience and hope. A student once shared that my positivity is infectious and that my smile goes a long way in bringing smiles to their faces. Another student recalled how the words I said during the last day of class - "Everyone has their own clocks and things will work out for each of us in the time it has to" - has kept her motivated to date. Whenever she fails a test – a job or otherwise, she remembers these words and forges ahead.

Students have come back to say my love for Derridean philosophy is contagious. It has inspired them to look beyond binary oppositions, explore new perspectives, question assumptions, and embrace the complexity of human experience. By introducing these concepts, I hope to cultivate in my students a love for deep thinking and a willingness to engage with difficult ideas. I take pride in witnessing students' "aha" moments, as they connect the dots between ideas and apply them to real-life situations. The aim has forever been to ignite a love for learning, fostering a lifelong pursuit of knowledge and growth.

When I had to write for this collection, I asked one of my students what he finds inspiring in my teaching, and his answer was simply, "You." I think this can be attributed to the "maternal vibes" my students affectionately mention and is part of my teaching style. Building relationships with my students is at the core of my teaching practice. I've been told that I exude maternal vibes, creating an atmosphere where students feel safe, warm, and nurtured. This connection, I believe, is crucial for effective learning. A student whom I taught both in UG and PG once told me that the fact that I don't talk to students individually but know each of them individually, and the fact that even the most introverted student in the class will get my attention, is something that inspired her. She mentioned that sometimes it felt to her that I'm reading the students' minds as I address the thoughts running in their minds almost instantly. I've always felt that when students feel supported and valued, they're more likely to ask questions, and engage deeply with the concepts taught in class. This telepathic connect sometimes extends beyond classrooms. An unforgettable instance is when I dreamt that one of my students was gloomy and sad, and I called the next day only to know that she was feeling desperate. This has happened to me more than once. Another student of mine said that whenever she feels sad or alone, I somehow end up calling her. I indeed feel that it's divine intervention that I could be there for these kids, not always though, in times of trouble.

As I write this reflection, I also remember those "full circle moments" when some of my students kept me motivated to overcome uncertainties and disappointments during my research days. This is why I strongly believe in the symbiotic teacher-student relationship. I'm also reminded of the countless moments that have made this journey so rewarding - the passionate discussions that spill over after class, the messages from former students sharing how our time together has impacted their lives, and my reflections on how they have enriched mine.

One of my students highlighted my leadership quality as emulable, noting how I lead without making anyone feel the pressure of it. He mentioned how I was able to bring out the best in the students while I headed the Literature association, resulting in a reference book, magazine, extension programme, and more, incorporating as many students as possible. He highlighted the dedication and integrity that is evidenced through my everyday activities and the respect that I give to everyone around by valuing their opinion, is something that brings out the best of the team I lead. This was indeed a revelation for me about myself as never have I considered to be an efficient leader.

Every day, as I stand before my students, I have aspired just to be a bridge between what is and what could be. In a world often divided by misunderstanding and fear of the "other", I strongly believe that we teachers have the power to build bridges of comprehension and compassion. Every word we speak, every concept we explain, every moment of patience we extend is a brick in the foundation of a more inclusive, empathetic, and enlightened society.

As I continue on this teaching journey, I have promised myself to remain committed to embracing the "other" within us, and steadfast in building a community of empathetic, optimistic, and inclusive individuals. If, in the years to come, my students both past and present, remember me as a person who encapsulated dedication, compassion, inclusivity, and empathy, I will know that I am journeying in the right direction. For these are not just qualities I strive to teach, but the very essence of what I believe education should be.

CHAPTER TWELVE

Troublemakers to Trailblazers

Pradeep P N

As educators, we often reflect on the profound and unexpected moments when we witness the transformation of our students. These instances are not just learning milestones for the students but for us, the teachers, too. They remind us of the immense potential young minds possess and the role we play in shaping that potential. My journey as an academician and entrepreneur has provided me with many such moments, and today I wish to share one of them—an experience that not only shaped two students but also transformed the entrepreneurial culture of a college campus.

A Journey Rooted in Social Work and Entrepreneurship

My journey into the world of entrepreneurship began long before I took on the role of a faculty member. I started my career as a social worker, collaborating with various non-governmental, governmental, and semi-governmental organizations. Over the course of 15 years, I had the opportunity to work across diverse sectors, conducting more than 100 skill training programs, focusing on youth and women's empowerment through entrepreneurship. These experiences provided me with deep insights into the power of entrepreneurship as a tool for social change.

However, when I pursued my PhD at Tata Institute of Social Sciences (TISS) in Mumbai, I noticed a stark contrast in how entrepreneurship was perceived in Maharashtra and Kerala. While discussions around business and startups were quite common in Maharashtra, Kerala appeared hesitant to engage in conversations about entrepreneurship. This disparity was perplexing to me, given that both states had vibrant, well-educated populations with immense potential. Upon completing my PhD in 2021, I felt a strong urge to bridge this gap and nurture an entrepreneurial mindset among young people, especially in my home state, Kerala.

Catch Them Young: The Beginning of a Mission

Upon joining Rajagiri College of Social Sciences in 2023, I was entrusted with coordinating the entrepreneurial activities on campus. By this time, I had accumulated a wealth of experience in entrepreneurship and training. Rather than returning to industry settings, I saw an opportunity to instill entrepreneurial values in students at a formative stage in their lives. "Catch them young," I thought. If we can spark an entrepreneurial mindset during their college years, they will carry that seed forward into their careers, making impactful decisions in the future.

I began this mission by launching a campus-wide campaign, "Let's Talk Entrepreneurship: Let's Create Enterprises." This became the slogan for our entrepreneurial initiatives and served as a rallying cry for students to engage in conversations about startups and business ventures. The idea was to create an ecosystem where students could freely express their ideas, take risks, and explore entrepreneurial possibilities.

The Case of Two Problematic Students Turned Entrepreneurs

One of the most memorable teaching moments from my tenure at Rajagiri College revolves around two students who were initially seen as "problematic." They were tarnished for disrupting class, engaging in deviant behavior, and generally being labeled as troublemakers. However, I saw something different in them—a drive that had not yet found its direction.

In my experience, not every student is academically inclined, but many have passions and talents that lie outside the traditional curriculum. As a teacher, it is our responsibility to identify these talents and channel them in the right direction. If we fail to do so, we risk alienating them, leading them to pursue unproductive paths. In the case of these two students, I recognized an entrepreneurial spirit in them—an energy that, if guided correctly, could result in something transformative.

From Deviance to Enterprise: A Transformation

I decided to take them under my wing, offering them guidance and mentorship. Slowly but surely, their energy was redirected from deviance to enterprise. Instead of disrupting classes, they became deeply involved in our entrepreneurial activities. Over the course of a year, they were not only participants in the programs but also emerged as leaders. Their involvement in entrepreneurship was no longer just an academic exercise; it became their passion and focus.

The impact of this transformation was profound. These two students, once seen as troublemakers, became the proud promoters of three startup initiatives from the campus itself. Their journey from disruptive students to young entrepreneurs was a testament to the power of mentorship, guidance, and channeling one's passions.

They frequently come to me for advice and guidance, no longer as troublemakers but as career-oriented individuals with a clear vision of their future. This transformation not only impacted their personal lives but also sent a powerful message to the rest of the campus—that entrepreneurship could be a life-changing journey for anyone willing to take the plunge.

Talent Hunts and Early Identification

This experience inspired me to introduce several new programs aimed at identifying and nurturing student talent from the very beginning of their college journey. We launched talent hunt programs where students could showcase their skills, be it in business ideas, creativity, or problem-solving. These programs allowed us to identify entrepreneurial talent early on, providing students with tailored mentorship and resources to develop their ideas.

Our goal was simple: to catch students at a stage where their minds were still open to new possibilities, free from the pressures of choosing a conventional career path. We wanted to plant the seed of entrepreneurship early so that when the time came—typically between the ages of 28 and 35—they would be ready to take the leap. At some point, we all face a decision: Do we continue working for someone else, or do we take the risk and build something of our own? By introducing entrepreneurship as a viable path early in their lives, we were empowering our students to make that choice with confidence.

The Role of Teachers in Nurturing Entrepreneurs

Reflecting on these experiences, one thing is clear: as educators, we have a crucial role to play in shaping the entrepreneurial journeys of our students. It is not enough to focus solely on academic achievements; we must also recognize and nurture the diverse talents and drives of our students. Whether a student is academically inclined or has a passion for business, art, or any other field, it is our responsibility to guide them toward fulfilling their potential.

Through my journey with these two students, I learned that entrepreneurship is not just about creating businesses; it is about creating opportunities for personal and professional growth. It is about recognizing that each student has a unique path, and our job as teachers is to help them navigate that path.

Conclusion: Building an Entrepreneurial Ecosystem

As Farrah Gray rightly said, *"If you don't build your own dreams, someone will hire you to build theirs."* Our role as educators is to guide our students in the early stages of their careers, helping them build their own dreams and empowering them to create their own path.

The story of these two students is just one example of the transformative power of entrepreneurship education. At Rajagiri College, we are building an ecosystem where students can explore their entrepreneurial interests, develop their skills, and receive the mentorship they need to succeed. Through initiatives like "Let's Talk Entrepreneurship," talent hunts, and personalized mentoring, we are creating an environment that fosters innovation, creativity, and a passion for entrepreneurship. As I continue my journey as an educator, I am committed to helping more students discover their entrepreneurial potential. My hope is that, through our efforts, we will inspire a new generation of entrepreneurs who will not only build successful businesses but also contribute to the social and economic development of our communities.

In the end, entrepreneurship is not just about building companies; it is about building dreams. And as educators, we have the unique privilege of helping our students build their dreams, one step at a time.

CHAPTER THIRTEEN

'Idendity' – Story of a Spelling Error!

Unnikrishnan P

By the time my research reached the opportunity stage, I had obtained a teaching position at Sri Sankaracharya University of Sanskrit and joined the Tirur Regional Centre in Malappuram district. Being my first teaching assignment, I was a bit worried at the thought of facing students as I joined the Tirur campus of the university in Malappuram district. I believed that I had a fairly good mastery over my subject, but still lacked the confidence to teach them. The first task assigned to me was to teach a class of 23 students on European philosophy. The fact that there were 10 girls in the class made me quite tensed! On those days, my preparation time was four to five hours for a class of one-hour duration! Slowly and slowly I gained confidence with the thought "I am a teacher."

While teaching, it was my habit to write the keywords on the blackboard. During one of my classes, I misspelt the word "Identity" as "Idendity". Most of the students wrote it down in their lecture notebooks. But one of the students who was sitting at the extreme back row took up his University identity card from his pocket and held it up for me to see the correct spelling of the word. I suddenly realized that I had wrongly spelt the word. He was not a studious student with an endearing nature, but he was very careful not to let his classmates see his efforts to help me correct my mistake. In no time I erased the scribbling on the board and wrote it down correctly again. It was the first setback to my vain feeling that I was a fount of knowledge and wisdom! I had to acknowledge the timely help of that student who took the initiative to point out the wrong spelling. My students might have realized that teachers are not infallible in their discharge of duties!

I was not sure if I had to announce the name of the student who pointed out my mistake, or not. The next moment I had the strong urge to openly admit my mistake and correct it. While thinking in that direction, unconsciously, I delved into the various connotations of the word 'Identity'. I came to realise that the majority of the teaching population lives with the false notion that accepting one's own mistake would bring discredit to their hard-earned fame and identity. They even force them to be controlled by the erroneous notion that 'teachers never go wrong'. My career as a teacher taught me that every teacher has to try to build up his/her own identity which invariably differs from that of others. I realized that a good teacher-student relationship can be strengthened only through giving and taking.

The lessons I learned during the early days of my teaching career gave me the realization that I should provide some space for my students to intercept, talk, share their ideas, and clarify their doubts during my serious lectures. I understood that the horizon of knowledge and wisdom widens only through continuous corrections. From then onwards I decided to practice the concept of "democratic teaching" in classrooms. Now, whenever I receive a "Teachers' Day" wish from my erstwhile students, I make it a point to thank them in turn for teaching me how to become a good teacher!

CHAPTER FOURTEEN

A Journey of Growth and Discovery in Teaching Literature

Jacob Alias

Teaching Literature has been more than just a profession for me—it has profoundly enriched, changed, and blessed my life in ways I could have never imagined. My journey as a teacher began with a deep love for books, but it quickly evolved into a profound dedication to my students' intellectual and personal development. Every day in the classroom feels like a fresh start, filled with the excitement of exploration, the challenge of deep analysis, and the joy of witnessing my students' creative and insightful responses to the literature we study together.

The moment I walked into my first classroom ten years ago, I knew I was taking on a significant responsibility. Each student I encounter brings a unique story and life experience to our discussions, which I see as invaluable assets. I strive to create a classroom environment that celebrates diverse perspectives, encourages critical thinking, and nurtures a genuine love for reading. My goal is to help students see literature not just as a collection of stories, but as a lens through which they can better understand the world.

One of the most rewarding aspects of teaching is witnessing the remarkable growth in my students. They don't just absorb information—they engage with it, developing their analytical abilities and beginning to see literature as a reflection of larger social, cultural, and historical forces. These moments of realization are the true testament to the impact of my teaching and bring me immense satisfaction.

Of course, the journey is not without its challenges. Keeping up with the ever-evolving canon of English literature requires constant learning and adaptation. Balancing the need to encourage critical thinking with the demands of academic success is a delicate act. Despite the effort this demands, the success and growth of my students make it all worthwhile.

One particularly memorable experience was when my students and I staged a production of *Dr. Faustus*. I had the opportunity to play the protagonist, and through this, I gained a deeper appreciation for my students' diverse talents—not just in acting, but also in backstage work, organization, and overall creativity. This experience was a powerful reminder of the multifaceted nature of learning and the unique strengths each student brings to the table.

Ultimately, the rewards of teaching far outweigh the challenges. The moments when a student connects with a difficult concept or offers a new interpretation of a text are incredibly fulfilling. These are the instances that reaffirm my passion for this field. Helping students develop their ideas, sharpen their arguments, and master the nuances of academic writing is a privilege, as it allows me to contribute to the growth of future literary scholars and thinkers. Seeing them evolve into confident, independent thinkers who can articulate their thoughts with clarity is one of the greatest joys of my career.

Teaching literature is about more than just imparting knowledge—it's about shaping minds, igniting curiosity, and fostering a lifelong love for learning. Creating an environment where students can learn to think critically and explore the world through literature is crucial in preparing them for the complexities of today's world. This journey as a teacher has been one of continuous learning, both for my students and for myself, and I look forward to the many years of inspiration and growth that lie ahead.

The road ahead is still full of opportunities and challenges. My passion for English literature remains as strong as ever, and I am eager to continue growing and evolving as a teacher. Teaching is not just a job—it's a calling, one that fulfills a deep-seated desire for knowledge and understanding. For that, I am incredibly grateful.

CHAPTER FIFTEEN

A Done-Day Ruminations

Allen Antony

"Maashe...!!"

I was stopped suddenly by a voice while walking out of the classroom. I turned to find Amina standing there, her mouth agape in disbelief. There was an embarrassment on her face which was intensified by the loud laughter of her classmates. She had made a slip of the tongue, accidentally uttering the word 'Maash' (a Malayalam word that stands for a teacher or someone who imparts knowledge), instead of 'Sir'! I glanced at my watch; it was 4:30 PM, and the dismissal bell had just rung.

As I strolled towards my cabin, I could see the white walls of the college painted orange by the rays of the evening sun; a warming sight that reminded me of my college days as a postgraduate student. Those were the days, I enjoyed, the quiet, satisfying sunsets spent in the serene 'lake view ground' of my college (SH College, Thevara), away from the madding crowd as the setting sun dipped below the horizon casting its reflection on the gentle ripples of the lake with slow winds brushing my hair. Being a hosteller then, I had enjoyed the privilege of countless sunsets immersed in solitary introspections on life, that were only put to a halt when the darkness spread slowly, with the birds perching on their nests and the people retreating to their abodes.

As the sky fills with the bells tolled from the nearby worship places, I too would return to my hostel room with my mind ruminating on various aspects, kindled by the theories and philosophies that have been offered in various academic papers to learn. I was happy indulging in private ruminations as I was at times reminded of Rene Descartes's famous maxim: "Cogito ergo Sum" (I think therefore I am /I am thinking therefore I exist). The ideas I had absorbed during my student days provided me with broader perspectives on life. Through introspection, I learned to listen to my inner voice, engage in inner debates and reach consensus, and that has become a part of my existence.

I sat in my cabin reflecting. The 'Course progression tracker' on my computer screen, devised to track the completion of the syllabus by teachers showed me the essay, 'Learning to be a Mother' by Shashie Deshpande to be taught next for a B. Com class. Through the essay, the author questions, decentres and deconstructs the glorified stereotypical image of motherhood. We see around a lot of instances of the glorified praises attributed to mothers and motherhood and the societal expectation of an 'ideal' mother on entering this phase in life. This glorified mother role that portrays mothers with a halo is a societal construct to remain conveniently blinded and unacknowledged towards their hardships and challenges. And, this idealized image of motherhood (the image of an 'ideal mother') affects, burdens, and conditions the mothers to carry out the societal expectation of executing this gender role, of being selfless, taking care of their husbands, family, and children while sacrificing their personal needs, private time and at times ignoring creative ambitions. A mother failing to fulfil these societal expectations will be considered a failure; a bad mother, and will be judged and stigmatized by the people around her, adding more insecurities, weaker mental state, and stress, often leading to one's insecurities thereby questioning one's abilities and existence. Deshpande challenges this "Special-ness" that confines their aspirations to motherhood alone. A self-loving mother, having time for her wishes and personal time and boundaries, who prioritizes her own needs over the family is considered selfish, and will face the question "How dare she! Isn't she a mother !?" People fail to think from their angle. The heaviness of the burden they put upon mothers deny the aspect that they are just ordinary human beings, they too have their desires, aspirations, and bodily needs and pleasures.

I had read the essay several times, and on reading the lines and between the lines at some point in my mind, the maternal metaphor gradually shifted to that of a 'teacher'. I could compare the image of an 'ideal' mother to that of an ideal teacher. Just like mothers, teachers are expected to be perfect and ideal, and are expected to fulfil every task that is imposed on them, denying them the space for their own personal needs, work-life balance, and self-care in the current challenging scenario. The old traditional concepts of teachers and teaching are dead. Today a teacher is not just a teacher; but a performer, clerk, entertainer, content creator, and so on, and is expected to meet all the expectations with an efficiency equal to that of a machine. Unlike other professions, teaching often requires extensive pre-work, in-work, and post-work preparation, extending the workday far beyond traditional hours. Taking a leave can be a significant burden for teachers due to the complexities of rearranging schedules, assigning classes, and potentially doubling their workload to catch up on missed content.

My mind flipped through a chain of thoughts - the trajectory of teaching is going through a changing and challenging phase. Teaching has undergone a seismic shift during recent years, particularly in the wake of the COVID-19 pandemic. Students' attitudes and expectations have evolved dramatically, influenced by the pervasive influence of social media and online platforms. The constant streaming of visually engaging content available at their fingertips has shortened their attention span, demanding educators to adopt more dynamic and entertaining teaching styles. Back offline, they demand the teachers to be of their 'vibe' and the ones failing will be stigmatized as 'boring' in the feedback which they consider an opportunity and autonomy to give tit-for-tat for the teacher's clutches over students.

Gone are the days of using the library as an area of personal and intellectual findings. There's a growing expectation that educators should provide students with all necessary materials and cater to their every need, eliminating any potential obstacles. In contrast to earlier generations who relied on library books and the internet to gather information and create personal notes, today students often expect to be spoon-fed with the content. This shift reflects a changing educational landscape where convenience and immediate gratification have become paramount.

Yes! It is in fact good that teachers need to change with time, improve and upgrade themselves with technology, but there are some virtues that are unaddressed – the foundational aspects of education! Students evolve and get prepared for real life through conditioning – from the family they grow up in, the teachers who help them to be better human beings nurturing them with knowledge and learnings, the books they read, the movies they watch, the peers they are influenced by, and so on. The lack of such conditioning that nurtures the students in their phases of growth can affect themselves and the people around them. Teachers have a great role along with the parents in moulding and developing students' character by influencing them. The students who are taught only about results and ranks, only about materialistic achievements and possessions, can only look at the world in terms of success and achievements – their lack of emotional development and empathy can make others' lives miserable, preventing them from living the lives they deserve. This kind of treatment, warmth, concern and appreciation are in fact little things that the students might cherish for a life.

Education should also be about making spaces favourable for other people; to make their lives liveable. We not only should equip students to be 'industry ready' but also ready for a life (that doesn't stop with one's career) with character development and life lessons. What the student receives from family, school, and college is carried along with them, they reflect the same, whether it be toxic traits or good things. They should be trained to be human beings and not workaholic machines, that are devoid of humane attributes.

The arguments and counter-arguments that happened in my mind were essentially about being a teacher in a changing epoch of time and it went too. My earliest memories of teaching are intertwined with my mother who was a high school teacher. Growing up, I witnessed the rewards and challenges of her profession. At times I recollect some perks of being a teacher through her: the cake pieces and chocolates she brought home in her tiffin box given by students on their birthdays, the evening snack served for meetings, the smell of library books that she brings home for us, the personal letters she received from her students, filled with gratitude and admiration; a treasured keepsake, the love and concern of her colleagues on visiting her staff room and the privilege of enjoying the title of being a 'teacher's kid'. It is through her that I have first experienced what makes teaching rewarding; the hearts won, the smiles exchanged along with greetings, the warmth of genuine conversations, celebrating cherished moments, witnessing growth, etc. which were in a way my primary motivation to be a teacher then.

Only after stepping into the role of a teacher did I fully comprehend the immense challenges teachers face daily. Maintaining composure and patience in the face of constant demands and frustrations is a formidable task.

We need teachers who inspire us to think critically, act compassionately, and live as fully realized human beings, rather than mere cogs in a machine-driven world. My mind conjured images of these genuine educators, many of whom were affectionately called "Maash." Amid all these streams of thoughts, I was reminded of Amina's call that belittled herself in front of her classmates. She had ordinary schooling unlike most of her classmates. It's true that we live in a society where respect often seems tied to one's achievements or social status, rather than inherent human value. This incident made me realize that the quality of education, while important, is not the sole determinant of personal growth. What truly matters is how education shapes us as individuals, fostering empathy, compassion, and a deep understanding of others.

We are currently in an epoch where the relevance of humanistic subjects, especially languages taught are undervalued. We are enchanted more by technology in the age of machines; we will miss such empathetic humane teachers who moulded their students fostering their holistic virtues. They are the ones who supported us, consoled us in our failures, gave us motivation, patted us on the shoulders whenever required, found out, and helped us to foster our hidden talents within. Amina stands as a metaphor- for the foregone traditional ordinary education, savouring the innocence, and cherishing the little things in life that wouldn't be valued in a fast world.

In the age of technology, the real predicament of a teacher would be to stay real, relevant, and humane, when you are expected to compete against the technology capable enough to replace them. Yet, there are qualities that no machine can truly emulate: – empathy, humanity, teaching through stories or one's lived experience, loving the students, and being kind and considerate.

As future generations become increasingly immersed in the digital world, these human qualities will become even more essential. The abundance of information and options available online can lead to a sense of detachment and isolation. Teachers, with their ability to connect on a personal level, can provide a much-needed counterbalance.

Even as we strive for efficiency and productivity, we must never lose sight of the importance of human connection. Teachers should be celebrated not for their ability to mimic machines, but for their unique ability to inspire, guide, and shape the lives of their students. What teachers expect is concern, encouragement, appreciation, and little acts of rewards that they can cherish for a lifetime.

As my collegues started leaving , waving hands at me , I wokeup from my thoughts; Awakening the computer screen that had gone to sleep, I logged in to Fedena to mark the student attendance. The next day Teacher's Day, a time when teachers are often idealized and showered with praise. However, I yearned for a more genuine recognition! As I teach my students 'Learning to be a Mother', I want them to learn to understand their mothers better – not as a person to perform the ideal mother role, and their other things but as a mother who wish to have fun and enjoyment; rather than being imprisoned in the societal image of a mother. Likewise on this Teacher's Day, I yearn for a more authentic recognition for teachers as well. Rather than idolizing us as infallible figures, I hope people would see us as ordinary individuals who are deeply committed to our students' well-being. It's not the grand gestures or artificial messages being sent that matter, but the simple acts of kindness and support offered while we struggle.

We are human beings trying to teach our students to be humane : not machines. Deshpande ends her essay thus: "I'm a human being first, a mother next". I too wish the same, the word 'mother' to be replaced by a 'teacher' Will that help? I like to think that it will.

.............................living their life for others

CHAPTER SIXTEEN

Prof. A.V. Ashok: A Man of Wisdom

Alex K. O

Indian tradition and culture teach *'Matha-Pitha-Guru-Daivam'* which means, along with a father and mother, a teacher also has a status that is equal to God. The reflection of a teacher as 'God' holds significance because, similar to how God established order and systems in the universe, a teacher shapes and frames an individual's life by instilling ideals and values, as well as imparting knowledge. As a result, a teacher bears a lot of responsibility, both as an individual and as a facilitator. That is why society attributes a godlike image to a teacher. During my time as a student, I had the honour of learning from exceptional teachers, including my university professor, Dr. A.V. Ashok. Professor Ashok was one of the most iconic and charismatic teachers at The English and Foreign Languages University. It was during the last years of my UG classes that I really began to notice this tall man with grey hair and a white *khaddar* shirt. He offered some of the best and most popular courses on our campus. As a result, the influx of students in his courses overwhelmed our normal classrooms, prompting him to hold his classes in a large hall near our undergraduate classrooms. This large crowd made me realize that when I become a postgraduate student, I must enroll in his course. Without any hesitation, I joined the same university for my post-graduation and enrolled in his 'Contemporary Non-Fiction' course. This course has changed my life and perspectives right from day one. Prior to this course, I used to read only limited prescribed texts in the syllabus, but this course introduced me to the magical world of nonfiction. Naturally, being a listener to Prof. Ashok's course and a reader of his prescribed texts, my language also began to change. Though he was discussing a whole book in parts due to time constraints, all those classes laid the foundation for me to build my reading habit. Until enrolling in this course, I was solely an average fiction reader, but this course transformed me into an avid reader of all works, including philosophy and nonfiction. The gradual and steady change in terms of reading improved my writing skills and broadened my imagination's horizons. In the semesters that followed this course, he taught us the poetry of T.S. Eliot, modern American fiction, and literary theory. All of these innovative English courses designed by Prof. Ashok have had a profound impact on my personal and professional lives.

It has been more than ten years since I have met him, but even now, when I read the poems of Eliot and see the names of Jonathan Shell, Hannah Arendt, and Steve Talbott, I still remember that outstanding visionary guru. Prof. Ashok used to say in our class that "what I teach today might seem irrelevant now, but in the future it will make sense." When I look back, he was absolutely right; now everything makes perfect sense. His words of knowledge and wisdom still lead my path, and when I fall into the depths of grief and pain, the books and authors introduced by him still provide comfort and consolation to me. It might seem a bit strange to say that I owe my life to a teacher, but based on the things that he has taught me and the kind of confidence he has instilled in me, I must say that this life is not enough to express my gratitude for all those memories and moments of wonderful learning.

CHAPTER SEVENTEEN

Experiences and Insights

Varghese S Nedumthallil

I believe, Teaching is the most noble profession. I quote Abdul Kalam Azad: "if a country has to become corruption- free,I strongly feel there are 3 societal members,who can make a difference – Father,Mother and Teacher". I firmly believe that the purpose of education is to mould good human beings with skill and expertise as Abdul Kalam reminds us.

While I was a school going student,my ambition was to become a teacher.I could manifest it in my life and it was an honour to be in the profession for more than 50 years including my teaching services even after my retirement.

My first step was an HSA in 1965 at Oniyan HS, Kodiyeri,a serene village five kilometres away from Thalassery. Myself and my friend Isaac got appointed there. It was a memorable step in my career as it was far away from my hometown. We started from Kothamangalam and reached the school on the eve of a fine Saturday. Gloomy night embraced the village. Being strangers, we couldn't get any stay facilities near the school.We occupied an open school room, which was not electrified.We lit a candle and joined together some benches to lay down in the night. During midnight, as sleep began to embrace me, I heard a vomiting sound of Isaac,who was suffering from diarrhoea.We were afraid of the contagious disease Cholera, which was prevalent in and around Thalassery Taluk. I ran to a nearby house. I knocked at the door and a gentleman came out. Fortunately he was Mr.Shivaraman,the attendant of Oniyan School. I explained our problem to him, and like a Good Samaritan he ran to a compounder, one Km away. Shivaraman came back with him and he gave Isaac some medicine. By the break of dawn Isaac was quite normal. It seemed he had food-poisoning. I still remember the striking words of Isaac.He appealed: "Varghese , you should inform my parents if I don't survive and kindly make arrangements for my funeral". I was in a dilemma because the communication facility we had on those days was very poor.

Another experience from the same school was an enlightenment in my life. Thalassery DEO was visiting Oniyan School for inspection. He entered my class seeking my permission while I was teaching English to students; he asked me to go on with teaching. Even though a little bit of anxiety developed in my mind, with a smiling face I continued my teaching. I was writing down some important words on the black board. After half an hour, the DEO left my class to inspect another class. During the lunch break the DEO called me and told me secretly: "Mr.Varghese you swallowed 'u' ,while writing 'Inauguration'. Now you may take it out and put it in the appropriate position". It was a gentlemanly correction, I felt. I rushed to the class in an affront mood during the lunch break while pupils were having their lunch. I noticed the word wrongly written on the board as 'Inaguration'! I advised the students not to swallow the food, but chew well. In the meanwhile, I corrected the spelling as *inauguration* and told my students to correct the word as in the board. I was grateful to the officer for correcting me.

Correlative teaching is my methodology. Once, while I was teaching 'AbhinjanaSakunthalam,' a drama by Mahakavi Kalidasa at St Peter's College Kolenchery, a psycho-analytic sloka in Act V had impressed me so much;

रम्याणि वीक्ष्य, मधुरांश्च निशम्य शब्दान्
पर्युत्सुको भवति यत्सुखितोऽपि जन्तुः ।
तच्चेतसा स्मरति नूनमबोधपूर्वं
भावस्थिराणि जननान्तरसौहृदानि ॥ २ ॥

It means' seeing pleasant things and hearing sweet sounds, even a person in the enjoyment of happiness grows concerned. It means that without his own consciousness he remembers the affinities of previous birth lurking persistently in his heart.

I detailed one part of the sloka in the class. Hearing sweet sounds now of an old song I go to that premises, where it was worked out. If I hear the film song now 'Arabikadaloru Manavalan, Karayo Nalloru Manavatti' (Arabian Sea the bridegroom, seashore the bride), in the radio or the TV, I would be going back to Dharmadam Seashore near Thalasserry, where the film Bhargaveenilayam (Ghosthouse) was shot in 1964, starred by Padmashri Prem Nazir and Vijaynirmala. I have witnessed this acting scene on the seashore 60 years ago. This recollection is due to 'Bhavasthirani Jananandara Souhrudani'. I could explain the depth and imaginary power of psycho-analysis by Kalidasa.

Yet another incident enhanced my impression about two foreign ladies – Ophera Gamaliel from Israel (now she is a Professor at Scotland University) and Anna from Russia. Both were research scholars in Sanskrit at The Sanskrit University of Kalady. They happened to visit St. Peters' College Kolenchery through the kind courtesy of Lecturer Ms. Sumi Joy, who is now the HOD of the Department of Malayalam in Maharajas College, Ernakulam. When Dora visited a literature class in St. Peter's College Kolenchery, she noticed the same sloka 'Ramyani Veekshya…' written by me on the blackboard. She recited it melodiously and legibly.

A moral lesson: the department of Malayalam took both of them for a picnic to Bhoothathankettu Dam over Periyar river. The Tapioca Biriyani tiffin brought by Lecturer Ms. Sumi Joy was our lunch beside the tranquil river bank. The spicy yet sumptuous food seemed to be uncomfortable for them and they were sneezing for a while. After lunch we left the banana leaf wrap somewhere around the river bank. To our surprise, Dora collected all the litters and deposited them in the dustbin near the river bank. We were ashamed of ourselves and I felt that the hygienic and responsible act of Dora was a moral lesson for me.

There were also a few bitter experiences in my professional life. Let me add two of them here. During 1995, I was selected as the Staff Advisor to the Elected College Students' Union. This non-statutory post was a selective one nominated by the principal at the interest of the Union Office bearers. Even though I was not aspiring for this position, few others were aiming for it desperately. In connection with the Union activities, renowned film star Jayaram was invited to inaugurate the Arts Club of the College Union. The Chief Celebrity Guest was late to reach the venue; meanwhile there came a phone call from the celebrity stating that he is not able to reach the program due to unavoidable circumstances. The Principal, Union Office Bearers & myself became panicked and the opposition group of students started to create a pandemonium among the crowd. To our surprise, the Celebrity Guest, Jayaram, reached the venue, though a little late, which we didn't expect after the call for cancellation. Hence, we enquired how did he make it to reach the venue suddenly; he was totally surprised and said he hadn't made such a call and we all learned that someone had deliberately mimicked his voice to create a problem.

Another situation that I recollect is; St. Peters College Staff Association organised a meeting to honour my disciple (Name not referred), as she was awarded Ph.D. for her thesis in Malayalam Grammar. Just before starting the function, a student (name not referred) was requested to buy a few bottles of drinking water at the cost of the department for placing on the dais. To my surprise the student refused and responded "I can't do it". Instead, a teaching staff bought the bottles. I was totally stunned by his behaviour and consoled myself that he represents the misbehaved modern young generation! No obligation; no obedience and lack of commitment to education and teachers. Contrary to the proverb-"Acharya Devo Bhava"!!

Now I may come back to my PG classroom in 2008. On the first day of the first hour of my MA classroom, I introduced myself and thereafter I asked, "Why did you opt for PG literature?"(Some of them were science graduates.)In general, they came to the conclusion that literature helps to develop the concept of identification, imagination and empathy. I asked one of my students, Sony (now Dr. Sony G., Assistant Professor at Rajagiri Arts College), what her name 'Sony' implies. She brilliantly answered that 'SONY' is derived from the Latin word SONUS, which means sound or music and in Malayalam the word for sound is 'sabdham' and the word for music is 'Sangeetham'. I really congratulated her for the insight.

Passion for teaching is a bliss and blessing' as I feel. It is better to become an effective teacher than an efficient teacher and a felicitator than a lecturer. I may conclude:" A good teacher can inspire your hope; ignite your imagination and thereby instilling love and learning"-Brad Henry

Best teacher teaches from the heart, not from the book.

CHAPTER EIGHTEEN

Thirty-One Years of Teaching: A Journey of Renaissance and Synergy

Sujeesh C K

On completing thirty one years of service as a teacher in an Aided College, one is sure to look back with mixed feelings, often keen to use superlatives.

I do take stock of the long experience among students with sense of contentment. I must, nevertheless, shoulder the responsibility of the thousands of students who slipped through my fingers, allured by tantalizing ideologies. I accept it; the responsibility, with pain and a patient shrug because thirty-one years of service in an Aided College implies accepting public money for a specific work and commitment. I have struggled hard to be worthy of the payment from the public exchequer.

Reminiscing one's long stint as a teacher, one tends to position oneself in the ideological bandwagon one has been riding on, belonging to one or the other teacher association with political affinities. I came out of the ideological fold (one joins one-fold while joining service) after my initial years, realizing that impartiality of the teacher is a charming necessity expected of the teacher by the large community of the young generation who look up to the teacher as they grow up. Impartiality of the teacher in a highly politicized society is a fantasy that most of the students appreciated.

Establishment of*Renaissance*: **Centre for Research, Extension and Studies in Literature and Arts** was in 2003-04 in the Golden Jubilee Year of the college; when I completed ten years in service. With the support of some teachers, the Centre started functioning with the objective of **Creatively Engaging the Young**. The work involved spending time among students, listening to their aspirations, planning some activities, executing and funding the activities. **"Study and Serve"** was adopted as the motto. As the students of Science disciplines also started participating in the informal gatherings and activities, a name change was effected:

Renaissance: **Multidisciplinary Centre for Research, Extension and Learning**.

When Renaissance completed twenty years of functioning, more than three hundred activities were completed by the Centre in schools and colleges across the state. Short films, nature trips, camps, exhibitions, theatre workshops, performances, reading sessions spread over many weeks, were some of the important activities. Participating in Seminars and attending the National level MUNs (Model United Nations) were also part of the engagement. The new members chalked out the list of activities for the year. The practice still goes on in the twenty-first year, 2024-'25. Renaissance Day is celebrated on 26 January every year - a happy reunion for the members. Needless to say, there is no exit for the members - once a member is always a member. This camaraderie would not exist but for the relentless work of the members of faculty Smt C. P. Lathika (Rtd) and Smt Sreedevi N. S.

Campus films: The Uniting Force

The chief objective of the Centre - "Creatively Engage the Young"- gets realized through the activities, especially through the filmmaking process. As film is a confluence of art and craft, many can contribute to its making. Film production is a symbiosis of many talents. The strategy of film making effectively effaces the differences among the members; binds them together as a responsible polity. Students belonging to different castes, religions, race tones, geographical and ethnic backgrounds, social and financial standings as a core team sit together, plan together, and work together. They first consider themes; and then narrow down on one topic of relevance and feasibility. The second stage is to prepare the script; and the third stage is the shooting. Shooting and post shooting stages are exacting, involving hard work and sacrifice. The launching of the short film is an occasion for the team to reminisce and enjoy the experience of work and fun which lasted for some months. The team work and the experience are more important than the film.

Under the leadership of a member from Kanhangad the team made a campus film on "thee theyyams", *Fire Theyyams*, which won many accolades. The shooting could be completed in two theyyam seasons, i.e, two years. It took three years to bring out the product, with three batches of members. When the annual system gave way to the semester system, the duration of films was reduced from thirty minutes to ten minutes or less. The present members have decided the topic for the film to be made in 2024-25 as "BLOOD!" Whether they would go for critiquing violence all over the globe or script the struggles of haemophilic patients is a point of anticipation for the coordinators.

Synergy: The Classroom Theatre

I would call this practice a marvel. Its form evolved through continuous interaction with the members. The first formal session was done in 2008. Soon, **Synergy** became well-structured and much sought after. *Nagamandala, Hayavadana,* and *The Fire and the Rain* by Girish Karnad, *The Glass Menagerie* by Tennesse Williams, *The Crucible* by Arthur Miller, *The Tempest, The Merchant of Venice, Macbeth,* and *Hamlet* by William Shakespeare, *The Accidental Death of an Anarchist* by Dario Fo, *Caligula* by Albert Camus, *The Emperor Jones* by Eugene O'Neil and *Doctor Faustus* by Christopher Marlowe were among the sessions presented as *Synergy*. The sessions have been held in almost all higher education institutions.

Hamlet remains the all-time favourite because the post graduate students of English find it a unique experience lasting for four and a half hours. I call *Synergy* a marvel because students of different disciplines attend the sessions. It is mystifying to see students sit through the 'no pen, no book, no mobile phone' sessions despite the fact that films based on the topics are available on the internet.

Why Synergy?

"Celebrate Learning!" Can this be a possibility? Conversations with the members often led to arguments and suggestions – some improbable and fantastic – so that classroom experiences sometimes be made celebration! At least occasionally, the teaching-learning process must be a celebration. The decision was made. The task to the teacher was set. To accept the challenge or runaway were the options. When the members in earnest place a demand, it is difficult to run away. Candour was our mode. After many discussions, the task was given a form – an introduction, followed by pieces of acting and analysis. *Synergy*: The Classroom Theatre envisaged as a celebration of learning with a combination of analysis and appreciation of the topic. "No pen, no book" policy was updated in 2015 as android phones became rampant; and "No pen, no book, no mobile phone" became the pre-condition for attending the session.

Each Synergy session required preparation that was time consuming. A first-time session requires preparation for months. A teacher's hands are full. Stretching extra is the only way out. Preparation for *Hamlet,* initially, took two years. Now it needs five days for preparation before presenting *Hamlet.*

The excitement and the starry-eyed enthusiasm of students are the motivating factors behind each *Synergy* session. At present, I am in deep contemplation: the members have given me the task of preparing *Synergy* on *Swapnavasavadatta* by Bhasa. I cannot fail them.

Higher education gravitates more and more towards research and publication, even at the expense of teaching-learning. But students too need some respite. Learning must be celebrated. Or a noble profession will cease to exist. Thirty one years among the students, spending time, energy and money, has assured me the worth of the teacher's total role to be among the students. After such knowledge, what forgiveness?

Not that, in my anxious detail of the many exuberant exercises I would be thought blind to certain flaws, which *a cunning carper might be able to pick in this Joseph's vest*. Notwithstanding, *Reniassance: Multidisciplinary Centre for Research, Extension and Learning* continues its work, ensuring a combination of creativity, love and sacrifice; the invigorating spirit being the '*Ashirvad*' of the members.

CHAPTER NINETEEN

Beyond the Veil – My Memories of Stage

Jithin John

Gone are the days of spot lights, experimentation, exhaustion, exhilaration and what not! It is my eleventh year as an English teacher at Baselius College, Kottayam. Walking down the memory lane is a poignant exercise, flashing a lot of 'etched memories' which evoke mixed emotions in me. Among the ripples, what stand out are the three performances done by our department and the endless discussions associated with the same. I would like to recollect the 'performance memories' which, I believe, played a major role in chiseling me as a teacher.

The idea of exploring theatre space in academics hit us in 2016 when I was in charge of the English Literature Association. I had engaged in a course on Drama, *Acts on Stage,* a compilation of different plays which emerged out of different literary, social and cultural fabric. During the discussion time, I felt that somewhere the nuanced perceptions of plays could not be inculcated in a usual classroom scenario. A lack of connection was felt by the whole group emphasizing the theorem- 'plays are written to be performed'. The discussion sessions in the classroom were enhanced by a performance session, where the plays were performed by the students' teams. Though my sole aim was to fetch some airs and premises of performance in the typical classroom space, I was awestruck by the way our classroom turned into a solid grueling creative space. *The Trick* by Erisa Kironde incarnated as a Shadow Play; *Matsyaganddhhi* by M. Sajitha was conceived and screened as a Short Film; Mrs. Rowland of *Before Breakfast* by Eugene O' Neil put as on the edge by her incessant wail so realistically, that we felt that we were in her two roomed apartments; *A Sunny Morning* by the Quintero brothers made the airs and our minds interestingly light. We never realized that theatrics had embraced our classroom and that we were the tensed performers and the responsible spectators. We shouted, cried and moved as characters; we clapped for our efforts. Needless to say, the texture and tone of academics took a new shade.

The enticement of the Performance experience called for new adventures. The Nirbhaya case was hot on the discussion tables even years after the callous crime. Like any Literature student may experience it, the new world of Feminism, Myth, Archetype and Psychoanalysis might have kindled their intellectual and empathetic sides. The discussions on the contemporary issues, gender sensitivities, myth and theatre culminated into the idea of a new play; that was how *The Marital Myth of Cleopatra* was sparked in the mind of Ajaikrishnan G., the then final year student. My major challenge was to identify the hidden mines of talent in the silent smiles and the non-pronounced presences in the class. I realised that this phase of selection is the most crucial part in putting the venture on rails. One of the students who used to dress up very aesthetically was told about the characters and I asked her how she would design the costumes for the character. A surprisingly detailed note of the costumes of each character with convincing rationale was a thing of joy to hear from an above average student in academics and one who keeps a low profile in class. The actors (especially those who didn't participate in the audition), dancers, technical hands- all came together creating a new dimension of collectivism in a profoundly moving way. *The Marital Myth of Cleopatra* depicts a museum where the personal possessions of a rape survivor were exhibited and how she breaks the shackles of her identity. The rehearsal camps were revelatory sessions where I witnessed the new gestures, body language and unseen skills of my students. The camps made us do away with the very formal aura of the teacher- student relation and evolved into a beautiful level of mutual comprehension. We sat, debated, danced, acted and had food together- understanding, learning and unlearning the politics and poetics of language, literature, space and body. The play was well received by the audience. We staged it again at Angamaly and Pala; the journey with the decked-up vehicle with the paraphernalia over it and identifying ourselves as the members of Urvasi Theatres in the movie *Mannar Mathai Speaking* brings a smile to my face even now. How time flies!

Matsyaganddhhi by M. Sajitha happened in 2019. After teaching the play, a few students came to me with the idea of staging *Matsyaganddhhi* for the English Literature Association (ELITA) Day. My proscenium nerves came out of their hibernation. The thought of an offstage performance of the play thrilled me once again. We gave a live sound for the performance. We included a pretext for the play with a group dance sequence highlighting the importance of the little narratives and the distinctiveness that stands beyond universal narratives. We compromised it to a small extent to include more students in the play, by bringing visual narration to the daydreams and tribulations the fisherwoman had to face in her daily life. I made it a point not to impose my concept of the characters' demeanor to the actors. Instead I curiously observed how they appropriated the characters to their comprehension and perspectives. From an amateur performer perspective, I thought that the priority was to experience the theatrical space rather than anything else. During a casual talk with my teacher, Rev. Fr. Shaji Puthenpurackal, I shared our humble co-curricular adventures which we believe would make the academic experience multi-dimensional. Father invited the team to perform in his school at Vaikom. The department designed it as our Extension Programme- "Education through Theatre". Amused were we by seeing the little tots and Upper Primary students as our spectators; quite unlike our usual audience at the college. The students performed it with such emotional honesty that after the play, a student came to the stage and emotionally shared her experience of how she had witnessed her grandmother (who was a fisherwoman) stood the social trials and stigma. We literally sensed the power of art and performance texts and left the school campus with full hearts.

It was the Diamond Jubilee year of our college and the Literature Association charge embraced me once again in 2023. This time we wanted to stage something in association with our Diamond Jubilee Celebrations. Quite incidentally, I watched the classic Malayalam film *Vaisali*, by the ace director Bharathan. I felt it incomplete as the climax of the film didn't show poetic justice to the character of Vaisali, though it resonates with many real-life experiences. *Vaisali-Her Quest*, the English ballet sprouts from this thought. What if there is an encounter between Lomapadha, the king and Vaishali after the climax! Anagha Mahesh and Sona P Varghese, our Postgraduate students and I tried to explore the untrodden paths of

Vaisali's mind. We realized that Vaisali's plight goes in tune with the "melancholic strain" of many lives marginalized by their castes and gender.

With the recorded voices of the characters, we tried the language of classical dance- *mudras, abhinaya* and *aangika* as the tools of performance. Two performers adept in classical dance performances played the lead role, supported by around twenty-five students on and off stage. The challenges were new to us, as the ballet was presented as an extension to the film text. We got convinced that off stage efforts are as important as the on-stage ones. For a play to be successfully staged, coordination, technical skills, presence of mind and talent should go hand in hand. After the play, many student acquaintances came to me and spoke to me with such vulnerability and emotional rawness. I felt content by seeing the sense of accomplishment in all the team members; we had written a new text too.

Teachers in the AI era are indeed relevant. I feel that with the advent of technology and invention of new appurtenances, teaching gets new colours; the horizon becomes broader and wider. The relation with all the students who became part of the play goes (obviously) stronger than the rest. Dr. Jyothimol P., my friend, colleague and Research Guide at M.G. University, Kottayam might have sensed my love for theatre. She encouraged me to pursue my research in "Theatre Studies" under her guideship, which is on its path now. At this point, as a teacher I'm grateful for the students for their trust in me, the department for the hands to hold, the college for its support and the stage for its magic in my life.

CHAPTER TWENTY

The Symphony of The Heart: A Teacher's Story

Dr. Sony G

Throughout my life, I faced many challenges on my journey to becoming a teacher. Since the time I can remember, it has been my wish to become a teacher. It was a big and distant goal to me, especially because I was not a naturally studious child. I did not enjoy going to school. I didn't even have a best friend during my school days. I was an introvert and preferred staying at home with my mother instead of going to school.

My mother would always tell me to study hard and secure a good job, but at that time, I ignored her advice. Still, the knowledge I gained from the classroom was enough to get me through with good marks. I am sincerely thankful to all my wonderful teachers who taught, supported, and guided me throughout my academic life.

After my marriage, I became very serious about my studies, and I went on to complete my B.A., B.Ed., M.A., M.Ed., NET and eventually my Ph.D. I earned all these degrees after my marriage with my family's unwavering support. This journey made me realise that nothing in life stands as an unconquerable obstacle when it comes to achieving our aspirations.

As a teacher, my aim is to be a guide to my students, just as my teachers were, to me. My students, even those I no longer teach, often call me to share their happiness, and whenever they face any difficulties, whether academic, professional, or personal, they seek my support and advice. I always keep in mind that the concept of teaching extends beyond the four walls of a classroom—it is about humanity. Just as I have the freedom to call my teachers at any time, I offer that freedom to all my students.

I truly believe that teaching and learning should not be confined to just the classroom but instead, it should resonate like a symphony throughout all aspects of life.

CHAPTER TWENTY-ONE

Being and Becoming a Teacher in Contemporary India: A Teacher's Perspective

Navami T. S.

The public and private universities in India are currently negotiating the transitions proposed by the National Education Policy (NEP) 2020. The past six to seven years have seen a major shift in the roles of administrators, teachers, researchers, and students. Moreover, the teacher is considered to be the center of the fundamental reforms in the education system:

"*The new education policy must help re-establish teachers, at all levels, as the most respected and essential members of our society, because they truly shape our next generation of citizens. It must do everything to empower teachers and help them to do their job as effectively as possible. The new education policy must help recruit the very best and brightest to enter the teaching profession at all levels, by ensuring livelihood, respect, dignity, and autonomy, while also instilling in the system basic methods of quality control and accountability. (MHRD 4)"*

Thus, the policy emphasizes maintaining the quality and accountability of the teachers or the faculty members in an academic institution. However, teachers in the contemporary global scenario of rapid technological advancements, digitalization, and the emergence of AI (Artificial Intelligence) tools encounter several workplace challenges. The role of a teacher and a classroom is constantly under scrutiny, following which they are forced to establish and explain to the students the significance and need of a 'facilitator' and a classroom in a world where everything can be gleaned from online and virtual sources, without even traveling from one place to another. Therefore, we must analyze and understand the challenges of being and becoming this new avatar of a teacher from the vantage point of the shifting academic culture in India.

Teaching has always been a multifaceted domain: it involves the academic development of students and teachers, it aims towards achieving a student's holistic growth, and it promotes the student's progress toward becoming a responsible citizen. The NEP 2020 also lays a particular emphasis:

"on the development of the creative potential of each individual. It is based on the principle that education must develop not only cognitive capacities – both the 'foundational capacities 'of literacy and numeracy and 'higher-order' cognitive capacities, such as critical thinking and problem solving – but also social, ethical, and emotional capacities and dispositions. (MHRD 4)"

However, 'the New Teacher' is expected to have a competent skill set with which they can 'engage' and mostly 'entertain' the students in new ways (although it is difficult to claim that the students have equally devised a competent learning method). 'Engaging the class' has become the norm for a teacher. 'Engaging' is a broader term in the context of the teacher-student dynamics in a classroom. It encompasses a teacher's teaching abilities, including their voice, tone, eye contact, appearance, and presentability; their knowledge and use of electronic and virtual tools while teaching and providing study material to the students; and their ability to control the students with the matter they teach, (and much more, depending on the demands of the department and the university). In addition to this, the teacher must constantly ensure that they have captured the students' undivided attention as their attention span has reduced so much as a result of the ongoing 15-second and 30-second content creation and content consumption patterns of social media. They need to cultivate novel pedagogical practices to retain the attention of the learners. Teaching has become a profession where one must constantly prove oneself to the 'stakeholders', who are the students, their parents, and the university. The students' feedback, other teachers' feedback, and the university's feedback declare if you are a competent or a 'good' or a 'better' or a 'best' teacher. The teachers are equally graded and evaluated akin to the students, and their salaries are affected by their 'performance' at various levels. The commodifying aspect of education has reduced a teacher to a facilitator and an entertainer who 'performs'.

This article calls for a primary inquiry to understand if the teachers are given enough space, time, and energy (both physical and mental) to devise such novel pedagogical practices and methods. After leaving a classroom, especially in private educational institutions, the students become a data set. Beginning from marking their attendance online, in addition to registering in hardcopy, to recording the evaluation details on MS Word and MS Excel, and uploading the paperwork online to the institute's virtual space, it devours enough time and energy to keep the teachers exhausted and distracted from the primary objective of their job, which is ensuring quality education to the students. The time and energy that should be dedicated to learning for the upcoming classes seem to be invested more in such mind-numbing clerical jobs, at least in a few academic institutions. Returning home after a long work schedule, there is very little time left for them to be with themselves and their family and then, prepare for the next day.

Thus, there is an urgent need to humanize the teaching profession. Devising a mechanism to increase accountability and ensure the quality of a teacher is as important as creating a healthy academic environment that recognizes the potential of and the challenges faced by a teacher. The educational system in India must understand that they can prevent the system from collapsing only by contributing towards maintaining the work-life balance of the employees. The NEP 2020 describes the role of a teacher as follows:

> "*Teachers truly shape the future of our children - and, therefore, the future of our nation. It is because of this noblest role that the teacher in India was the most respected member of society. Only the very best and most learned became teachers. Society gave teachers, or gurus, what they needed to pass on their knowledge, skills, and ethics optimally to students. (MHRD 20)*"

It is pertinent to acknowledge the fact that the teachers are no 'super-entities' who go back to their cloisters or pods; they are human beings who have a social existence, have a family, have a personal life with desires and pleasures, and have their own identities. It was only two years ago, in August 2022, that a female teacher was forced to resign from a leading private university in Kolkata, India, because she posted her private photos on Instagram (Pandey, 2022). Thus, the divine altruistic aura with which a teacher is visualized must be changed. Instead of perceiving them as 'noble' spirits, they must be perceived as humans in flesh and blood who require adequate wages, physical and mental well-being, and rest and recreation to achieve a quality life. Akin to any other profession, there is a strict need to ensure "quality service conditions and empowerment of teachers" (MHRD 20) as proposed by the NEP 2020 so that the best possible future for "our children and our nation" (20) can be ensured.

.

.

References

- MHRD. *National Education Policy 2020*. Government of India, 29 July 2020, www.education.gov.in/sites/upload_files/mhrd/files/NEP_Final_English_0.pdf. Accessed 25 Aug. 2024.
- Pandey, Geeta. "Kolkata St Xavier's Teacher: 'I Was Forced to Resign over Bikini Photos.'" BBC, BBC News, 20 Aug. 2022, www.bbc.com/news/world-asia-india-62601044. Accessed 25 Aug. 2024.

CHAPTER TWENTY-TWO

Lessons that Last

Aishwarya Paulson

Haim Ginott, an Israeli Educational Psychologist in his book *Teacher and child; a book for parents and teachers* critiques education with the below quote, which is in a letter format addressed to teachers:

> "*Dear Teachers:*
>
> *I am a survivor of a concentration camp. My eyes saw what no person should witness. Gas chambers built by learned engineers. Children poisoned by educated physicians. Infants killed by trained nurses. Women and babies shot and burned by high school and college graduates.*
>
> *So I am suspicious of education. My request is: help your students become more human. Your efforts must never produce learned monsters, skilled psychopaths, or educated Eichmanns. Reading, writing, and arithmetic are important only if they serve to make our children more human.*"

This quote is part of the first introductory session I have with my students to imbibe in them the true spirit of education, and it has also personally driven me to go beyond the criteria of grades and to create a meaningful impact in the lives of my students.

This reminds me of the experience I had with one of my students in the beginning phase of my career. A very well-built, hot-tempered child who would repeatedly land in fights with classmates and was categorized as a troublesome kid. The instances of strict disciplinary actions from authorities were normal routine in his case. A similar incident happened in my class which proceeded with a personal interaction with him which he reluctantly obliged and later his parents being summoned to discuss their ward. The interaction with the parents was an eye opener for all of us as we then realised the problem wasn't with the child but his parents, especially his father.

It so happened that the father dashed into the Principal's office demanding the reason for them being called in the local language. The Management seeing the response and the behaviour of the parent was very much willing to terminate the admission of the student but we pleaded for the student. Later on with again an attempt at a casual talk with the child did we realise the way the family including his mother and siblings were being physically and mentally abused by the father who was also a local goon. All the anger suppressed by the child towards his father was displaced towards his classmates, unfortunately his only outlet. Correcting his father was not in our hands, but didn't want to miss out with this child. So slowly and gradually we started working with the child and saw a sea change within a year.

I did leave the institution shortly afterwards, but what surprised me was a sweet note from this child after he completed his course enquiring after my well-being and thanking me for playing a vital role in his life to quote his words "changing him from an animal to a human" and sweetly addressing me as Akka(elder sister). The icing on the cake was when he informed me the good news of him being offered a position in the same institution. This incident made me realise the privileged role we play in a student's life with the capability to make or break them.

The thought of being a teacher had never once occurred to me even in my far-fetched dreams, not because I wasn't fond of the profession, but because I never imagined myself to be capable of the same. Now when I look back I am filled with gratitude to the Almighty, parents and teachers who moulded me into the person I am and the profession I am passionate about and consider as my vocation. Especially here I would like to mention Dr. Seema Bhaduri Ma'am, who was the Head of the Department, when I was pursuing my graduation and post-graduation from H.P.T College. Ma'am was the teacher who instilled in me critical thinking as an English Literature student, practically making me think from multiple angles and question different perspectives.

The most valuable lessons I learnt were not in the class scenario but mostly in the personal interactions I had with my teachers. In my journey of learning, I saw my teachers becoming my guides, friends, mentors and philosophers. These are the qualities and legacies I would like to carry forward through my vocation. In the present context, teaching Gen Z and Gen Alpha in a digitally advanced era with a very short attention span has got its own hurdles especially in the post-covid scenario, but I do believe that such challenges carve out a better version of the teacher to shape forth thinking individuals. I hope that the lessons I learnt and would like to impart to my students wouldn't sum up with the summative exams but will be something that lasts for a lifetime.

CHAPTER TWENTY-THREE

Building Relationships with Students to Foster their Development as Better Humans

Joji John Panicker

Dreams, much like seeds, require a conducive climate and environment to germinate and flourish into towering trees. True education is the cultivation of a generation that aspires to great visions for society and commits itself wholly to realizing those aspirations. In the prevailing educational paradigm, the emphasis frequently rests on academic success, standardized assessments, and the acquisition of technical expertise. However, education today is not merely evolving but undergoing profound transformation. Globalization has ushered in a new world order, where corporate interests increasingly influence the educational landscape. This shift often stifles creativity and critical thought among learners. Yet, the essence of education transcends the mere transmission of knowledge and skills; it involves nurturing individuals who are responsible, empathetic, and morally conscious members of society. At the heart of this endeavor lies the vital relationship between educators and students, a bond that shapes the future of learning.

Building meaningful relationships with students transcends being a mere pedagogical strategy for enhancing academic performance; it constitutes an essential element in nurturing their growth as empathetic, responsible, and ethically conscious individuals. Such connections form the emotional and social bedrock upon which students can evolve into more complete human beings, armed with the virtues and competencies required to navigate an increasingly intricate world. Educators hold a pivotal role in shaping the moral and intellectual trajectory of society, and by investing in the relational dynamics with their students, they help cultivate a generation committed to compassion, justice, and integrity. It is through these profound relationships that education fulfills its loftiest aim: the development of individuals who are not only learned but also deeply humane.

The Philosophical Foundations of Relationship-Building in Education

Education is often conceptualized as a process aimed at actualizing the latent potential inherent within individuals, with the teacher-student relationship serving as its pivotal element. The ancient Greek philosopher Socrates posited that true teaching extends beyond the mere conveyance of knowledge; it is a dialectical process characterized by inquiry and reflection. The Socratic Method, in particular, rejects rote memorization in favor of a dynamic approach where students are guided through probing questions, encouraged to engage in self-examination, and empowered to discover knowledge from within themselves. Within this philosophical paradigm, the relationship between teacher and student is not merely transactional but deeply relational. The teacher's role transcends that of a mere instructor to encompass that of a guide, mentor, and often a moral exemplar. In such an environment, students are more likely to flourish, feeling genuinely seen, valued, and respected.

Students demonstrate increased engagement and motivation when they perceive their teachers as understanding, respectful, and valuing their individuality. This relational pedagogy fosters a transformative educational experience, allowing students to move beyond superficial learning to develop deeper connections with the subject matter, their peers, and themselves. Educators who embrace this approach place equal emphasis on intellectual development and the nurturing of students' moral and emotional growth. These educators leverage personal interactions as opportunities to instill values such as respect, responsibility, and empathy. By integrating character education into their relationships with students, they cultivate individuals who are not only academically adept but also socially and ethically aware, prepared to contribute meaningfully to society.

Building Trust through Authenticity and Vulnerability

A fundamental aspect of cultivating meaningful relationships with students is the teacher's authenticity. Students, with their astute perception, are often quick to recognize whether a teacher is genuine or merely performing a role. Authenticity builds trust, and trust is the cornerstone of any significant relationship. When educators allow themselves to be vulnerable, openly acknowledging their own mistakes or sharing their personal learning experiences, they create an atmosphere of safety and transparency. In such an environment, students feel encouraged to respond in kind, fostering a mutual openness that deepens the learning experience. This focus on authenticity is closely aligned with Paulo Freire's educational philosophy, which advocates for a pedagogy rooted in mutual respect and co-learning. Freire rejected the traditional, hierarchical model of education in which the teacher functions as the sole authority dispensing knowledge to passive students. Instead, he championed a dialogical approach where teacher and student engage in a collaborative learning process. In this model, both parties contribute to the exchange of ideas, creating a dynamic interplay that transcends mere knowledge transmission.

In a classroom that values authenticity and dialogue, the role of the teacher shifts from that of an authoritative figure to that of a facilitator and co-learner. This transformation fosters a culture of shared responsibility and mutual respect, essential ingredients for both personal and intellectual growth. When students see their teachers as human, fallible, and engaged in their own ongoing learning, they are more likely to embrace the learning process themselves with curiosity and resilience. Furthermore, this approach cultivates a deeper sense of agency in students, empowering them to take ownership of their education and recognize the value of their contributions. In such an environment, education becomes a transformative, rather than transactional, experience—one that nurtures not only intellectual development but also emotional and ethical growth. Teachers, by embodying authenticity, help students see that learning is a lifelong process, rich with challenges, reflections, and personal insights. This relational foundation ultimately helps shape individuals who are not only knowledgeable but also empathetic, self-aware, and prepared to navigate the complexities of the world with integrity and confidence.

The Impact of Teacher-Student Relationships on Character Development

The relationships teachers cultivate with their students often transcend the confines of the classroom, leaving a lasting imprint on students' lives well into their future. A teacher's influence is particularly profound in shaping character, as the moral and ethical values imparted through these interactions can resonate far beyond the academic sphere. Research consistently demonstrates that positive teacher-student relationships correlate with numerous beneficial outcomes, including enhanced academic performance, improved social competence, and greater emotional regulation. By modeling positive behaviors and creating a classroom environment that emphasizes values, teachers help shape the ethical and moral compass of their students.

At the heart of this dynamic lies character education, an essential dimension of the teacher-student relationship that emphasizes the nurturing of moral virtues and ethical principles. Whether consciously or unconsciously, teachers serve as role models, exemplifying the values they seek to instill in their students. Their actions, words, and treatment of others offer daily lessons in respect, responsibility, empathy, and integrity. Through consistent modeling of these values, educators subtly influence the character development of their students, shaping their moral compass. This influence extends beyond the immediate learning environment, as students carry these lessons into their interactions with others and their approach to challenges in life. By embodying the virtues they promote, teachers contribute to the formation of individuals who are not only academically prepared but also equipped with the moral foundation necessary for responsible citizenship and ethical leadership in an increasingly complex world. The relationship between teacher and student, therefore, is not merely a conduit for intellectual growth but a vital force in shaping the character and future contributions of the next generation.

In the formative years of my teaching career, I encountered a student named Thomson who exhibited a reserved disposition and faced challenges in forging connections with his peers. Recognizing Thomson's isolation and anxiety, I endeavored to integrate him into group activities and cultivate a sense of belonging within the classroom environment. I also dedicated time to engage with Thomson individually, demonstrating a genuine interest in his thoughts and emotions. Through these concerted efforts, Thomson gradually exhibited increased comfort and confidence. I entrusted him with a significant responsibility—coordinating a National Level Intercollegiate festival—which he executed with exceptional proficiency. This responsibility not only showcased his capabilities but also served as a testament to the effectiveness of personalized support and encouragement. The supportive and inclusive environment I strived to create was instrumental in Thomson's transformation into a more engaged and self-assured individual.

This experience underscores the profound impact that personalized attention and a nurturing relationship can have on a student's character development and overall self-esteem.

Gandhian Philosophy: Education for Life

Mahatma Gandhi's educational philosophy, encapsulated in his concept of "Nai Talim" or "New Education," presents a holistic approach that integrates the head, heart, and hands. Gandhi envisioned education as a transformative process that goes beyond mere literacy and academic learning to foster the comprehensive development of individuals—intellectually, morally, and physically. His approach was grounded in the belief that education should prepare individuals not only with essential life skills and ethical values but also with a profound sense of social responsibility.

In his Basic Education Scheme, Gandhiji argued that education should transcend vocational training and aim for the holistic development of the person. From the very beginning of a child's educational journey, Gandhi advocated for the inclusion of practical manual skills. He believed that engaging in such skills contributes significantly to personal growth and character development. According to Gandhiji, the effective training and engagement of the sensory organs are crucial for the proper development of intellectual faculties. Active sensory involvement, he posited, accelerates and enhances cognitive development, thus enriching the learning experience.

Gandhiji's vision for education also encompassed the pursuit of the highest form of learning, which he defined as the attainment of wisdom and self-awareness. He famously asserted that "true education is that which teaches us to know ourselves," suggesting that self-knowledge represents the zenith of intellectual achievement. Gandhi envisioned education as a means to cultivate morally conscious individuals who are critical thinkers, steadfast in their commitment to truth, and courageous in their pursuit of justice.

For Gandhiji, the process of personality development involves a deliberate effort to purify oneself, removing the impurities and deficiencies imposed by a world fraught with inequities. Gandhian education, therefore, is both a quest for truth and a path to liberation. Gandhiji argued that education serves dual purposes: to preserve an existing world order if it is just, or to reform and revolutionize it if it is not. He emphasized the latter, advocating for a transformative approach to education rather than a mere preservation of the status quo. Rather than rejecting contemporary educational reforms outright, Gandhi urged for the infusion of critical thinking and the pursuit of alternative lifestyles within the existing system. He envisioned education as a continuous process of renewal, advocating for teachers to embrace this renewal as a mission. Gandhiji's insight guides us in this endeavor, asserting that "a handful of good-hearted people, with unshakable faith in the mission they have undertaken, can indeed influence the course of history."

Mahatma Gandhi also highlighted the profound impact of the teacher-student relationship, stating, "I have always felt the true textbook for the pupil is his teacher." This underscores the importance of teachers serving as exemplars of the values and principles they wish to impart. For Gandhi, a teacher's life should reflect the values they teach, including integrity, ethical conduct, and a commitment to lifelong learning and personal growth. He believed that teaching transcends mere occupation; it is a vocation of character, where the teacher's conduct and personal example are paramount.

In essence, Gandhiji's educational philosophy calls for a deep, personal engagement between teachers and students. He envisioned teachers as mentors who guide students not only in academic pursuits but also in their personal and ethical development. In the contemporary Indian context, where education is often reduced to rote learning and examination preparation, Gandhi's vision serves as a reminder of the importance of nurturing compassionate and responsible human beings through education. His philosophy advocates for an education that shapes individuals into not only knowledgeable citizens but also ethical and empathetic members of society.

The Importance of Setting High Expectations with Compassion

A pivotal aspect of fostering meaningful relationships with students lies in striking a delicate balance between setting high expectations and demonstrating compassion. It is vital for students to feel that their teachers hold a deep belief in their potential and are committed to challenging them to reach new heights. However, these expectations must be framed within a nurturing environment, where students understand that failure is not a measure of their worth but an integral part of the learning journey. Teachers are instrumental in cultivating this mind set by setting ambitious goals while simultaneously providing the support, encouragement, and empathy necessary for students to meet them. In doing so, educators create an atmosphere where rigor and compassion coexist, empowering students to develop resilience and a deeper sense of agency in their own learning process.

I had a student named Derin who faced a significant personal crisis during his studies. Instead of focusing solely on academic guidance, I took a keen interest in understanding Derin's broader life goals and aspirations. I provided mentorship that extended beyond the academic realm, encompassing career planning and personal development. Over time, Derin came to regard me not merely as a teacher but as a trusted advisor and role model. My support and encouragement were instrumental in helping him gain clarity regarding his future and build the confidence needed to pursue his aspirations. Years later, as a successful professional, Derin continues to regard my mentorship as a pivotal influence in his personal and professional development. This experience exemplifies the profound impact that teachers can have on shaping their students' lives, transcending mere academic achievements.

Conclusion

Recognizing the diversity of learning styles and needs, educators can adopt personalized learning strategies that address each student's unique strengths and challenges. By investing time in understanding each student's individual capabilities, teachers can offer tailored support and mentorship. This personalized approach not only enhances academic performance but also deepens the connection between teacher and student, fostering a more engaged and supportive learning environment. Furthermore, by emphasizing character education and ethical behavior, teachers play a pivotal role in shaping students into conscientious and responsible individuals capable of making positive contributions to society. This is especially pertinent in the Indian educational context, where education is often narrowly focused on academic achievement. Teachers who forge meaningful relationships with their students can profoundly influence their holistic development, addressing not just intellectual growth but also emotional, moral, and spiritual development.

Drawing inspiration from India's rich educational traditions, such as the Guru-Shishya dynamic and Gandhian ideals, modern educators can create an environment that nurtures compassion, integrity, and responsibility. By overcoming challenges such as large class sizes, curricular pressures, and entrenched cultural norms, Indian educators can work towards a more relational and comprehensive educational experience. Ultimately, the true purpose of education extends beyond merely producing academically successful individuals; it is to cultivate well-rounded human beings who contribute positively to the welfare of society. Teachers, as mentors and guides, are integral to this transformative process, shaping the hearts and minds of future generations and steering them toward a more just and compassionate world.

In conclusion, fostering strong relationships between teachers and students is crucial for creating an environment where students feel safe, valued, and included. This entails cultivating a classroom culture steeped in respect, empathy, and open communication. Teachers should encourage students to voice their thoughts and concerns without fear of judgment, ensuring that every student, irrespective of their background or abilities, is treated with dignity and respect.

CHAPTER TWENTY-FOUR

Holistic Research Development: The Library's Role in Shaping Academic Excellence

Vijesh P.V, Vishnudas A V, Suryagayathri

Introduction

Academic libraries have long been more than storehouses of books and other informational materials, but if Wakefield is any guide they must remain dedicated to the daily pragmatics. Now, they have become vibrant hubs supporting research and are integral in enhancing academic excellence through 360-degree Research Development. Academic libraries serve as the engine for academic and scholarly pursuits by supplying critical resources, services, and expertise that structurally enable faculty members to succeed in their teaching excellence (Basu, M. (2020). Conducting Your Research Libraries are at the very core of research, contributing in multiple dimensions from access to comprehensive information resources and facilitation services through critical research skills, ethical practices and collaborative opportunities.

The idea of holistic research development involves more than "how to" access libraries and archives or use digital tools — but also encompasses teaching rigorous empirical methods, critical thinking about data sources used in historical scholarship (that is telling a story based on fragments), coupled with principles of ethical research practices. The additional academic library services provided in these processes, such as information literacy training, custom research assistance and help to cope with the growing informational challenges, will allow the coming generation of scholars to perform their own evaluation in an ethical manner. Besides, electronic libraries have contributed to further enhancement of resources through development of online digital repositories as part of the library system infrastructure and open access which provides the accessibility to research resources and transparency.

Research is a key component when it comes to pursuing an academic career since it brings about not only knowledge but also innovation and growth in minds (Adeleke, A. A., & Olorunsola, R. 2010). In addition, students and faculty members are able to enhance their critical thinking, problem solving and general understanding of their respective disciplines through the act of researching. Nonetheless, research is not an easy task to conduct and it is resources concerning support systems that make the difference in why an academic library is important in an institution. In this regard and by virtue of the two, in the promotion of knowledge sharing, in provision of research activities, access to scholarly materials, the role of the academic library performs two roles: (i) enhancing individual productivity while also maintaining the overall productivity of the faculty in order to enhance the scholarly output of the institution.

The Accreditation Milestones of Rajagiri College of Social Sciences

Rajagiri College of Social Sciences (RCSS), established by the Carmelites of Mary Immaculate (CMI), is a pioneering institution in higher education in Kerala. Inspired by St. Kuriakose Elias Chavara, the CMIs manage a vast network of educational institutions across India, including RCSS. Founded in 1955 as the first college in Kerala to offer a Masters in Social Work (MSW), RCSS has expanded to provide 17 programs, including Management, Computer Science, Library and Information Science, and Behavioral Science, across its Hill and Valley campuses in Kochi. RCSS is affiliated with Mahatma Gandhi University and has earned recognition for its academic excellence, state-of-the-art infrastructure, and global partnerships. Rajagiri Centre for Business Studies (RCBS) represents the college's management programs. Committed to its motto, "Rajagiri, Relentlessly towards Excellence," RCSS continues to produce globally competitive graduates while upholding values of love, truth, and justice.

The NAAC Accreditation of Rajagiri College of Social Sciences is as follows:

1st Cycle (2000) - 5*

2nd Cycle (2007) - A+

3rd Cycle (2013) - A Grade (3.70 out of 4)

3rd Cycle Extension (2018) - A Grade (3.70 out of 4) upto March 2020

4th Cycle - A++ Grade (3.83 out of 4)

Rajagiri College of Social Sciences (RCSS) has consistently demonstrated excellence in quality education, as reflected in its NAAC accreditation history (Dalrymple, P. W. 2001).. In its 1st Cycle (2000), the college was awarded 5 stars, followed by an A+ rating in the 2nd Cycle (2007). In the 3rd Cycle (2013), RCSS achieved an impressive A Grade with a score of 3.70 out of 4, which was extended in 2018 with the same score until March 2020. Most recently, in the 4th Cycle, the college earned an exceptional A++ Grade with a score of 3.83 out of 4, showcasing its continuous commitment to academic excellence.

National Institutional Ranking Framework (NIRF)

2024- Ranked 20th in College Category

2023- Ranked 30th in College Category

2022- Ranked 27th in College Category

2021- Ranked 31st in College Category

2020- Ranked 28th in College Category

2019- Ranked 35th in College Category

Rajagiri College of Social Sciences (RCSS) has shown a strong upward trend in the National Institutional Ranking Framework (NIRF) over recent years. In 2024, the college achieved an impressive ranking of 20th in the College Category, improving from 30th in 2023 and 27th in 2022. Prior rankings include 31st in 2021, 28th in 2020, and 35th in 2019. This consistent improvement reflects the college's commitment to academic excellence and its growing reputation at the national level.

Fr. Moses library

The Library of Rajagiri College is named as Fr. Moses Library, which is named after Rev. Fr. (Dr.) Abraham Moses CMI, first principal of the Rajagiri College of Social Sciences. In order to conserve and share information with the academic communities, the college library was established in 1981. The library offers extensive collections of books, magazines, periodicals, national and international journals, professional studies, PhD thesis, dissertation, project reports, annual reports, conference proceedings, news documents, etc.

Subscribed Databases and softwares

Fr. Moses Library offers a comprehensive suite of online databases and software to support its academic community. The library provides access to **Elsevier SciVal**, which offers advanced analytics and research performance metrics; **ScienceDirect**, a leading full-text scientific database; and **Emerald Insight**, renowned for its business and management content. Researchers can also utilize **IEEE Explore** for extensive engineering and technology literature, and **ACM Digital Library** for computing and information technology resources. **NLIST** and **DELNET** offer access to a wide range of digital resources and inter-library networking services. **J-Gate Plus** enhances access to electronic journals, while **Turnitin** supports plagiarism detection and ensures academic integrity. These resources collectively enhance the research capabilities and academic success of the library's users (Adeleke, A. A., & Olorunsola, R. 2010).

Services provided by the library General Services:

The general services provided by the library are as follows: book lending services, interlibrary loan, reference service, user orientation service, magazines and newspapers, R & D service, SDI Service, binding and lamination service, reprography service, Proficiency center, CONFAB – Information Discussion hall, Current awareness service (in the press today), Documentation services, Technical consultancy service, Property Counter, Lift services.

ICT Enabled services:

The ICT enabled services provided by the Library are: Wi-fi access at a speed of 100 Mbps, Web-Enabled auto-lib integrated library management software, a web-based software package with SMS modules, and Email notifications, a database search feature online, and an information navigation centre (41 systems altogether), Bar-code technology for the circulation of documents, Web OPAC (Online Public Access Catalogue), Journal Content alert service, Library Web 2.0 tools (Library blog, social networks etc), Access gate (E-gate register), Digital Repository (Dspace), New arrival alerts service, Special service for visually challenged users, In the press today – daily news service, Conference alert service and Professional training.

Library extension services:

At the beginning of each academic year, it includes user orientation workshops and library awareness services. Brochures about the library and user instructions are given to the users.

External Extension services:

External extension services provided by Fr. Moses Library are as follows: campaigns for book donations, services for academic and non-academic libraries in the area of library consulting exhibitions and book fairs, and initiatives for libraries in schools and colleges. Library consortium (Mikitish, S. 2017) to bring together the knowledge of a number of libraries, to share resources, and coordinate activities. Fr. Moses Library also offers reference services to aspiring researchers and academics from outside, orientation activities, and tours of the library.

Role of Fr.Moses Library in Holistic research development

The main category of users of the library contains Undergraduate and Postgraduate students, faculty members of different departments, research scholars from the departments of social work, computer science and psychology, and other teaching and non-teaching staff of Rajagiri College.

Research and publication are crucial for academic institutions as they provide deep insights into fundamental questions about human- social existence and institutions. The primary aim is to uncover and understand various facts, their interrelationships, and to advance our grasp of reality while addressing distortions. Through research, we gain valuable information about the nature of social and educational institutions, which helps in managing social phenomena and assessing current needs and developmental stages. Research also identifies and critically examines pressing issues such as social stratification, gender inequality, poverty, and unemployment that impact educational systems. Additionally, it plays a vital role in proposing practical solutions and innovative strategies to tackle these challenges. It addresses the root causes of existing problems in research facilities, and the implementation of effective corrective measures, thereby driving progress and improvement in both academic and societal contexts.

Higher education relies on research due to the need to resolve discrepancies between actual practice and desirable outcomes, the process which assists in identifying the existing shortcomings in both research and learning. It promotes the comprehension of other areas of study as well as their different core elements which leads to further inquiries and creativity in coming up with new concepts. It is noted that in the domain of social sciences, research is ever beneficial concerning society, social structures or educational establishments through encouraging research, examination, and integration of changes. When research outcomes are used in the course of instructions and learning in schools, several issues regarding learning can be resolved including the effectiveness of teaching strategies. Furthermore, research guides the training and practice of teachers, curriculum reform, and education systems along with enhancing the growth of teachers professionally. It equips professionals with the ability to teach and prepare their students for the 21st-century and change their mode of instruction to embrace research and particular theories.

Research combo facility for enhancing research productivity

The Fr. Moses Library is committed to the improvement of the educational process and improvement of the output of research with the help of a complicated research combo facility. The library in this case has and uses such information indexed databases as Emerald, Elsevier SciVal, IEEE, JGate Plus which make it possible to retrieve vast information from the academic literature and other research materials. In addition, *Turnitin* helps in adapting the originality of the work and enhances original scholarly works and *Quillbot* performs language and grammar correction. This comprehensive solution allows for a cyclical research process: databases are mined by users; *Turnitin* is used to check the originality of the documents, and *Quillbot* is used to edit the documents. With the combination of these very essential tools and many others, the ability of users of the Fr. Moses Library to be efficient and effective in all their research work has been enhanced as they receive adequate assistance in all the phases of some research work they are conducting.

Earn While You Learn:

The library offers an internship program called "Earn while you Learn" to Department of Library and Information Science students. Students apply for the position of "Library Trainee," and one student is chosen following an interview process. After that, he or she receives proper guidance in a number of areas, including stack verification, circulation, technical, and cataloguing. Daily work at the library will be done by the chosen students after their regular classes. On weekends, they are also able to work. A stipend is awarded to them based on the number of days they work.

Different Dimension of ICT (Information Communication Technology) Services

Current Awareness Services

A practice that has drawn a lot of attention is "In the Press Today," a service that distributes information from print and electronic newspapers that the library subscribes to. Stories concerning the subjects- education, scholarship and finance are selected, which have an impact on the faculty and students of RCSS. They are distributed by mail to every RCSS student and faculty member.

Academic Alerts

Focus Group - Faculty

It's a new initiative that has begun this academic year, where the focus group is faculty and the IQAC team. Under this initiative, we gather important circulars and notices published in various government portals, specifically UGC, AICTE, MHRD and Kerala Higher Education. These are circulated among the respective faculties under the title- UGC INFO ALERT, AICTE INFO ALERT, MHRD INFO ALERT and Kerala Higher Education Alert through mail.

Focus Group- Students

An alert service titled "SCHOLARSHIP ALERT" is provided from the library to students. In this service, students receive information about scholarships that they are eligible for over mail.

WhatsApp

The Library team closely interacts with students through Social Media Platform. Here we have formed a WhatsApp group where a student representative of each programme is added and from here we provide up to date information regarding the library services. It includes providing updates of newly purchased books and databases list, Library rules and timing etc. This information is passed to their respective classmates.

Instagram Handle

The library team intends to launch an Instagram account in order to reach a wider audience and promote library's resources and services. We also hope to enhance communication with our patrons, who include students, staff, researchers, and others.

Future Plans:

The library team intends to launch an Instagram account in order to reach a wider audience and promote library's resources and services. We also hope to enhance communication with our patrons, who include students, staff, researchers, and others.

Lantern

Lantern is a collaborative initiative between Library and Information Science Department, Language Department and Library, where we select students from various departments to narrate the summary of novels, short-stories that they have read. The videos are tapped from our college studio and are uploaded to our YouTube page. The next stage of this initiative is to upload videos where students interact with each other on various topics that are relevant to their respective courses.

Library Notice Board

The Notice Board placed in various floors of the institution is the next project we look forward to, the boards will hold informative clips – that includes information regarding Library Rules, Latest Database System Purchased, Seminars, Conferences and Webinars initiated by Library or Department of Library and Information Sciences. Etc.

Conclusion

Fr. Moses' Library at Rajagiri College of Social Sciences plays a vital role in the enhancement of a holistic approach towards the growth of research as well as academic excellence. Considering this aspect, the library encourages active research by making available a variety of resources such as e-resources, research tools and other specialized services which include information skills training. Other methods like academic alerts and contents from the social media of the library and the Lantern project aid the professional and academic development of the students and faculties respectively. The research potential of its users is also enhanced by ICT based facilities of the library such as digital and online libraries. It is trying to incorporate more services like Instagram marketing and better ways of interacting with the users, Fr. Moses Library is an example of library services with a concept ahead of its time. Such a commitment to the changing patterns of the research demands gives it a central place in fostering the academic and the research needs of the society thereby promoting a continuous learning environment.

Bibliography

- Adeleke, A. A., & Olorunsola, R. (2010). Training in the use of e-resources in academic libraries: One university's approach. *Library Hi Tech News*, 27(6/7), 16–19. https://doi.org/10.1108/07419051011095872
- Basu, M. (2020). Importance of Research in Education. *SSRN Electronic Journal*. https://doi.org/10.2139/ssrn.3703560
- Connaway, L. S., Harvey, W., Kitzie, V., & Mikitish, S. (2017). Academic library impact: Improving practice and essential areas to research.
- Dalrymple, P. W. (2001). Understanding Accreditation: The Librarian's Role in Educational Evaluation. Portal: Libraries and the Academy, 1(1), 23–32. https://doi.org/10.1353/pla.2001.0004
- Fountain University, Osogbo, Osun State, Nigeria, & Adeola, B. M. (2014). Accreditation and the Role of the Academic Library in Undergraduate Programs: A Case Study of Fountain University, Osogbo. IOSR Journal of Humanities and Social Science, 19(10), 45–48. https://doi.org/10.9790/0837-191034548
- Joseph, F. F., & Urhiewhu, L. O. (2016). Roles of Academic Libraries in University Accreditation in Nigerian: Challenges and Way Forward. 6.

- Kavithanjali, J. (2019). E – Resources: Their Importance, Types, Issues and Challenges: An Analysis. 6(1), 4.
- Kenchakkanavar, A. Y. (2014). Types of e-resources and its utilities in library. 9.
- Padval, D. B. S. (2022). E-Resources: Definition, Need and Types. 7(5), 3.
- Sharma, C. (2009). Use and Impact of E-Resources at Guru Gobind Singh Indraprastha University (India): A Case Study. 12.
- Ullah, A., & Usman, M. (2023). Role of libraries in ensuring quality education at higher education institutions: a perspective of Pakistan. *Inverge Journal of Social Sciences*, 2(4), 13-22.
- NAAC website: http://naac.gov.in/index.php/en/
- NIRF ranking: https://rajagiri.edu/about-rankings
- Rajagiri webpage: https://rajagiri.edu/
- Fr. Moses library website: https://rajagiri.edu/library

CHAPTER TWENTY-FIVE

Evaluating Teaching Practices: Concerns, Obstacles, and Factors to Consider

Sada Warsi

Reflective practice has emerged as a key term in teacher education, signifying a level of professional skill. It is often seen as a type of repetitive and organized investigation where educators meticulously gather data on their teaching methods to examine, make sense of, and assess their experiences with the goal of enhancing their future instructional practices (Farrell, 2016a; Mathew & Peechattu, 2017). It serves as a process of making meaning that allows educators to develop (Rodgers, 2002). Reflective educators seek not only to find more effective solutions but also to gain a deeper understanding of themselves and the ways in which the solutions they uncover relate to other experiences and concepts. Indeed, the importance of reflective practice has been consistently acknowledged (Loughran, 2002; Yalcin Arslan, 2019). As indicated by the research, reflective practice plays a crucial role in transforming two primary aspects of educators' professional lives: their sense of identity as teachers and the quality of their teaching.

The concept of teacher identity refers to how educators perceive themselves as both individuals and professionals (Mockler, 2011). This concept covers both the personal and professional sides of a teacher's identity. Specifically, for aspiring teachers, it's crucial to develop a deep understanding of themselves and how they fit into the broader educational environment, as this significantly impacts their effectiveness in teaching. Engaging in reflective practice is essential for fostering this understanding (Beauchamp & Thomas, 2009). Essentially, reflective practice offers teachers a chance to examine and improve their feelings, beliefs, and personal teaching philosophies (Walkington, 2005). For instance, Slade et al. (2019) explored how a teacher candidate's perspective on her students' academic progress changed after maintaining a reflective journal for roughly one semester. The study revealed that upon realizing her students' struggles with poverty, which were affecting their academic performance and behaviour in the classroom, the teacher became more empathetic towards them. This research supports Korthagen's (2017) claim that reflective practice helps novice teachers recognize their own thoughts and feelings.

Challenges in Implementing Reflective Practice in Educator Training

Based on a study of literature, the concept of reflective practice has evolved gradually. The initial stages of its development were marked by shifts in the approach to reflective practice, while the later stages focused on the method of reflective practice itself. Additionally, the study advises teachers to proceed with caution when applying reflective practice in practical teaching settings.

Development of the Reflective Practice Framework

While discussing the concept of "reflective practice," two key theorists, Dewey (1933) and Schön (1983), have offered foundational ideas to foster a unified understanding of the term. Dewey views reflective practice as a methodical process of thinking where educators utilize insights from their past experiences and their knowledge or beliefs to make informed decisions about their teaching, rather than making hasty decisions based on habitual patterns. In essence, Dewey sees reflective practice and problem-solving as closely related activities. Schön (1983) further expands on Dewey's ideas by incorporating the element of time into the reflective process, suggesting that reflection can occur both after an educational experience (reflection-on-action) and during the teaching process (reflection-in-action). Schön suggests that educators use their reflections to inform their future teaching practices based on their understanding of past experiences. These foundational ideas have been integral to research on reflective practice for many years; however, they are somewhat limited in their scope and fail to fully capture the complexity of teachers' professional lives. Teachers explore their teaching experiences with the goal of identifying and correcting their mistakes (reflection-as-repair, as described by Freeman, 2016).

Development of the Reflective Practice Process

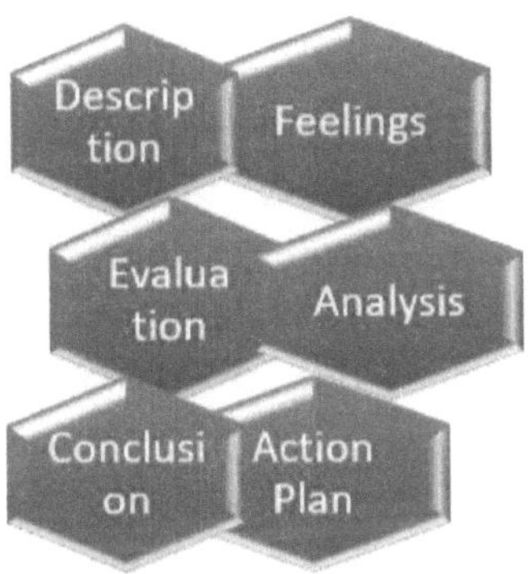

Figure 1

In terms of implementing reflective practice, in-service educators might struggle to understand the process of reflection. This section introduces three frameworks that can assist and "support" the reflective journey in teacher education.

The framework was initially presented by Gibb (1988) and is organized in a sequence as depicted in Figure 1.

This six-phase structure illustrates the ongoing growth of in-service educators' reflective thought processes. The six phases are outlined in the following sequence:

Description: At this phase, aspiring educators are prompted to reflect on the intriguing event that sparked their interest or desire for deeper comprehension. They are then required to outline the specifics of the scenario. It's crucial for these aspiring educators to refrain from forming any opinions or reaching any inferences regarding the event.

Feelings: In this stage, pre-service educators delve into the thoughts or emotions they experienced during the event. They are not allowed to form any conclusions or evaluations, but they must recognize the influence of the incident on their thoughts and emotions.

Evaluation: Future educators in training can assess the positive and negative aspects of the event, also taking into account the strengths and weaknesses of others involved. They should acknowledge this, even if the event appears to be entirely negative.

Analysis: Educators in training can defend or evaluate their behaviour using their current understanding, scholarly works, or viewpoints from others.

Conclusion: Before they begin their teaching careers, pre-service educators merge their past reflections to make reasoned inferences about their newly acquired knowledge or potential alternative actions.

ActionPlan: Taking into account the earlier phases of the process, pre-service educators propose a strategy for enhancement in a comparable scenario.

Figure 2

The framework created by Korthagen and Vasalos (2005), suggests that educators can grasp the true essence of a situation only when they personally engage in self-reflection and have the chance to delve into their own identities as educators. In this approach, Korthagen and Vasalos liken the process of reflection among pre-service teachers to peeling an onion, starting from the outermost layer and moving inward.

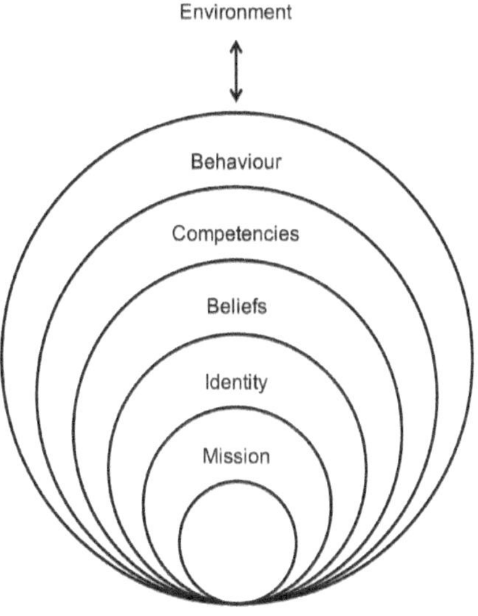

Figure 2

The initial layer is where pre-service teachers examine the obstacles they encounter; the second layer deals with how they address these obstacles; the third layer involves contemplating solutions to these challenges; the fourth layer focuses on their perceptions and beliefs about these challenges; the fifth layer reflects on their self-perceptions; and the final layer is where pre-service teachers consider what motivates and gives purpose to their lives or their careers.

Figure 3 Displays the final structure, introduced by Farell (2015), designed to create an all-encompassing model that integrates every element of reflection, including both the intellectual and cognitive dimensions of teaching, as well as the non-cognitive elements of the inner world of pre-service teachers.

This model is organized into five tiers: philosophy, principles, theory, practice, and beyond practice.

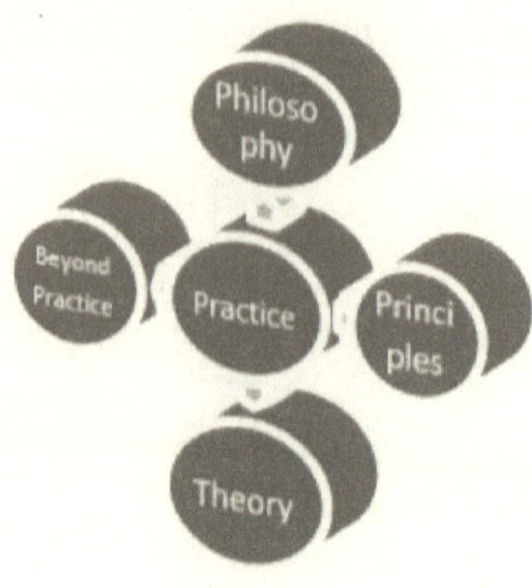

Figure 3

Philosophy: The aim of this phase is for pre-service teachers to contemplate their past and life experiences before entering the service. They develop a deeper understanding of their identity as they gather details about their history.

Principles: Educators-in-training think deeply about their possibilities, convictions, and understandings of instruction and education. In doing so, they start to question if these concepts are applied effectively in actual classroom settings.

Theory: At this phase, pre-service educators need to review the strategies, instructional activities, and instructional approaches they select to determine if they can effectively implement them in a classroom setting.

Practice: In this phase, future educators review the visible behaviours of both themselves and their students. Through watching their own teaching and that of their students, future educators can explore whether their behaviours in the real classroom align with their thoughts and theories from the reflection and principles stages.

BeyondPractice: At this point, aspiring educators are motivated to investigate and analyze the ethical, political, and societal factors that shape their teaching methods both within and beyond their educational environment.

The aim of this article is not to determine the most effective framework, but rather to examine the various aspects of reflection highlighted in each one. By doing so, teacher educators or supervisors can choose the framework that suits a specific situation, as well as the reflection skills and needs of their future teachers. Finlay (2008) argues that future teachers should not be exposed to just one framework for reflection. Rather, they should understand that various frameworks can lead to different degrees of reflection, and each framework should be applied thoughtfully and in the right context.

Ease in Adopting Reflective Practice During the Teaching Internship

The teaching practicum, also known as teaching practice, field experience, or internship, has emerged as a crucial element in today's teacher education programs (Zeichner, 2002). It acts as a link between the theoretical knowledge and practical application, enabling aspiring teachers to put their academic learning into practice in actual classroom environments. Consequently, these future educators develop a deeper understanding of teaching in real-world scenarios, identify the needs of their students, and become aware of the challenges they might face in their teaching careers (Smith & Lev-Ari, 2005). However, the teaching practicum is also recognized as a particularly challenging period for aspiring teachers, marking their first formal teaching experience. The aspiring teachers in Jusoh's research (2013) reported numerous difficulties during their teaching practicum, including difficulties in applying theoretical knowledge to practice and a lack of support from professionals. As a result, these future teachers often feel overwhelmed by stress and fear, including fears of failure and uncertainty (Harscher et al., 2004). These challenges are not unique to aspiring teachers from a single culture but can be experienced by those from diverse backgrounds (e.g., Chinokul, 2012; Nguyen & Baldauf, 2010). Given the difficulties and challenges faced by aspiring teachers during their teaching practicum, it becomes clear that this period is an ideal time for the development of reflective practice, as reflection often starts in response to these challenges.

Obstacles in Implementing Reflective Practice in Educator Training

During the reflective practice process, in-training teachers may face several obstacles, which are outlined as four primary inquiries, with their solutions detailed as follows.

Guidelines for Encouraging New Teachers to Reflect Before Starting Their Jobs

There are a variety of methods that aspiring teachers can use to reflect on their practice, including keeping reflective journals, engaging in group learning, documenting lessons, observing their peers, and more. However, this discussion focuses on reflective journals, as they are a common practice in teacher education (Jaeger, 2013). Keeping reflective journals can be advantageous for aspiring teachers in several ways. Primarily, it enhances their self-awareness. Farrell (2016) suggests that writing in a journal is a reflective practice that enables teachers to pause and consider their thoughts, then review what they've written, and finally, to reflect on their insights, which can lead to a deeper understanding of their professional life. Goker (2016) carried out a research project with 16 aspiring teachers in Turkey, who were asked to maintain reflective journals about their teaching experiences over a semester. At the conclusion of the semester, the participants were interviewed about their experiences with journal writing. The results indicated that journal writing increased the participants' understanding of their teaching methods and how to evaluate them.

Steps to Advance Your Reflection Skills

Despite the numerous advantages that reflective journals bring, the act of writing in them is not always perfect. In research conducted by Bell et al. (2012) and McGarr and Moody (2010), a notable problem identified was the tendency of pre-service teachers to prioritize the volume of their journals over their quality. They often write lengthy, superficial accounts of their classroom activities without engaging in meaningful reflection. Indeed, reflective journals that are dominated by descriptions of classroom activities are seen as ineffective and do not align with the purpose of reflective journals, which should serve as a catalyst for thought. To tackle this issue, it's important to consider both the scope and depth of the reflection process (Tiainen et al., 2018). Scope is about the content of the reflection, which includes various elements related to personal experiences, emotions, teaching in the classroom, and social contexts, while depth refers to the interpretation and analysis of this content (Thompson & Pascal, 2011). For pre-service teachers to develop into reflective practitioners, they need to delve deeper into situations with a more analytical perspective. Therefore, it's crucial to explore how to enhance the depth of reflection. The existing literature offers several frameworks that can help teacher educators and supervisors guide the reflective process of their pre-service teachers.

Effects of Reflective Practice on Teacher Identity and Teacher Excellence

Farrell (2003) has outlined the challenges that first-year teacher trainees face, describing their experience as a "sink or swim" journey. This term highlights the obstacles and frustrations they encounter, prompting two essential questions that aspiring teachers must address to develop their professional identity (Graham & Phelps, 2003). The initial question is "Who am I?" and the subsequent one is "What am I expected to do?" Finding answers to these questions can assist aspiring teachers in understanding the relationship between their personal identity and their approach to teaching. Thus, educational programs for future teachers should aim to equip them with the necessary resources to explore and comprehend their external environment, including the educational institutions and classrooms they will work in, and how these elements may influence their journey towards becoming educators

(Trent, 2010). Engaging in reflective practice is a crucial approach that helps future teachers align with their personal identity and deepen their comprehension of their working environment.

Conclusion

In conclusion, this piece emphasizes the role of reflective practice in supporting aspiring teachers in their professional journey. Engaging in reflective practice requires an understanding that it's not just about addressing issues in classroom instruction but also about paying attention to the personal development of pre-service teachers. The piece delves into various reflective models without favouring one over the other, suggesting that pre-service teachers should gradually be exposed to these models due to the absence of a universal approach. The challenges identified in the research highlight critical issues that teacher educators need to be mindful of when incorporating reflective practice into their teaching methods. The article concludes by discussing the potential of technology in improving reflective practice in the digital age and the impact of reflective practice on the identity and teaching quality of pre-service teachers.

References

- Arms Almengor, R. (2018). Reflective practice and mediator learning: a current review. Conflict Resolut. Q. 36, 21–38. doi: 10.1002/crq.21219
- Ai, A., Al-Shamrani, S., and Almufti, A. (2017). Secondary school science teachers' views about their reflective practices. J. Teach. Educ. Sustainability 19, 43–53. doi: 10.1515/jtes-2017-0003
- Aliakbari, M., and Adibpour, M. (2018). Reflective EFL education in Iran: existing situation and teachers perceived fundamental challenges. Eurasian J. Educ. Res. 18, 1–16. doi: 10.14689/ejer.2018.77.7

- Babaei, M., and Abednia, A. (2016). Reflective teaching and self-efficacy beliefs: exploring relationships in the context of teaching EFL in Iran. Austral. J. Teach. Educ. 41, 1–27. doi: 10.14221/ajte.2016v41n9.1
- Cirocki, A., and Widodo, H. P. (2019). Reflective practice in English language teaching in Indonesia: shared practices from two teacher educators. Iran. J. Lang. Teach. Res. 7, 15–35. doi: 10.30466/ijltr.2019.120734
- Childs, A., and Hillier, J. (2022). "Developing the practice of teacher educators: the role of practical theorising," in Practical Theorising in teacher education: Holding theory and practice together. eds. K. Burn, T. Mutton and I. Thompson (London: Taylor & Francis).
- Choy, S. C., and Oo, P. S. (2012). Reflective thinking and teaching practices: a precursor for incorporating critical thinking into the classroom? Online Submission 5, 167–182.
- Georgii-Hemming, E., Johansson, K., and Moberg, N. (2020). Reflection in higher music education: what, why, wherefore? Music. Educ. Res. 22, 245–256. doi: 10.1080/ 14613808.2020.1766006
- Grant, A., McKimm, J., and Murphy, F. (2017). Developing reflective practice: A guide for medical students, doctors and teachers. West Sussex, UK: John Wiley & Sons.
- Goodley, C. (2018). Reflecting on being an effective teacher in an ageof measurement. Reflective Practices,Vol,19,pp,167-178.
- Huda, M., and Teh, K. S. M. (2018). "Empowering professional and ethical competence on reflective teaching practice in digital era," in Mentorship strategies in teacher education. eds. K. Dikilitas, E. Mede and D. Atay (IGI Global), 136–152.
- Meador, D. (2017). The most essential qualities of a good teacher [Blog post]. Retrieved from https://www.thoughtco.com/the-most-essential-qualities-of a-goodteacher EffectiveTeacher Characteristics: Future Teachers' Voices Gavrielle Levine, Ph.D. NERA 2017

- Priya Mathew, Prasanth Mathew, Prince, J. Peechattu 2017. Reflective Practice: A Means to Teacher Development. Asia Pacific Journal of Contemporary Education and Communication Technology, 3 (1), pp 126-130.
- Sellars, M. 2012. Teachers and Change: The Role of Reflective Practice. Procedia- Social and Behavioral sciences. 55, pp 461-469.

CHAPTER TWENTY-SIX

Teacher's Odyssey

Dr. Susan Sanny

In a classroom packed with enthusiastic eyes
From senior secondary to college halls
I've watched them grow and blossom exquisitely
Amidst the hustle and bustle, I wound my way
Ready to sow the seeds of knowledge
To nurture ideas and unlock potential
To kindle the flame of curiosity
To touch each life with the lessons taught
To interweave dreams of the future.

Teaching English, a skill, an art
In each young mind, I've etched a mark
Role plays brought stories to life
Interactive sessions cut through the qualms
The flipped classroom, a twist, a turn
Where students achieve erudition
Through syntax rules and literary musings
I've woven words into lifelong leitmotifs
To engross, enthuse and set minds free
Has been the core of my legacy.

Twenty-eight years' stint, the time flies

Together we reckoned the ripostes
In these classrooms, stories spun
Years of laughter, moments of ambiguity
The world sketched in profound thoughts
Each lesson unfurled a canvas rare
Daubed with fortitude, love, and care.

And as I look back, the memories blend
From the least triumphs to ostentatious goals
In every pupil's journey, my heart exalts
For in their progress, my purpose is found
And as the bell tolls
I carry with me the tapestry of a teacher's odyssey.

CHAPTER TWENTY-SEVEN

Memory by the Water

Surya P. Nair

Shimmering water touched her toes as she stooped slightly, sitting with her feet slung down the edge of the pier. Water hyacinth swayed vigorously and tadpoles danced. The ripples of the Arabian sea shone above the home of multi-coloured fish. It was in 1988, four years after Priya's retirement. Ducks waddled by, heading for Sadasivan's courtyard. She felt like a toddler again, observing quaint birds, peering at sea creatures, staring at unattended Chinese fishing nets and matching the energy of the island breeze.

The barnacles had not aged since then. A little farther, live prawns glistened, making her feel like one of the mermaids visualized in the secluded reading rooms of elementary schools. At those moments, Priya perceived herself underwater, though the swimming lessons had ended prematurely. The see-through shrimp glinted and she rued the fact that the industry turned them into opaque meat. Adulthood had seen her embracing the global wave of vegetarianism.

Priya's family that familiarized her with the pier was no more – Grandpa who fought in the war but spoke nothing of his adventures till the end; Grandma who forgot words in the final years, after teaching generations of village schoolchildren, and many other departed kin. When her memory served her right, Priya remembered events exactly as they had occurred, even the clothes they wore on that occasion, and the scent of Radhas or Moti soap to which they were partial, or the smells of cooking, depending on the time of day. Now, those days were prolonged on which she could barely remember her own name.

She had learnt to walk on these very shores. As a little girl, Father had held her hand on sandy Middle eastern trails. It had been half a century since he was no more, but was remembered the most by his wife. Priya's profession took her on long walks in the melting snow of the Himalayas, the farming heartland of North Karnataka and the congested settlements of Delhi. Her present meanderings all ended at the pier. Everyone on her particular island of Cochin knew Priya as the retired teacher who lived alone and was fast losing her memory.

She heard the leper, singing tunefully while begging on the approaching passenger boat. The usual crowd emerged on the boat jetty. Only one man appeared different from the local populace. He was tall, gaunt, sunburnt and distinctive. This man stood ramrod straight and walked with a majestic gait. The step was slightly unsure only at the left knee. "Ah!" she thought to herself, "posture and injury from a military career." He retained a boyish air, though on the threshold of middle age.

"Good afternoon, Priya ma'am, I am Sahasranshu Sen. I was in your class of '63 in Delhi Cantonment. They said I could find you here."

"Are you sure? Priya ma'am...Delhi Cantonment...not ringing a bell. You know, my mind plays tricks nowadays. I should really not be out here, talking to new people."

"I am not one of the *new people*, Ma'm. You really don't remember me, SS, do you? I used to sit on the front bench, waiting for your class although the rest of the boys made noise as you were lenient. The other teachers barely saw me in the early days, unless there was some mischief. You drew me out of my shell. Speaking Hindi was difficult. I got the gender wrong for most words, so I was silent. Then you came to our school, noticed me and coaxed answers out of me in English. Wanted to thank you in person all these years but got your address only after retiring from the army."

"SS – I was fond of him, but you are someone else. Not able to find any resemblance. The complexion, the jaws, the voice, everything is different. I waited for news of him but none came. Assumed he had a remarkable life somewhere, and prayed for his success whenever I thought of him. He was a gem. SS wouldn't have become a soldier. Who are you really, young man?"

"I am exactly who I claim to be, Ma'am. Father had a clerical job but many responsibilities and financial liabilities. So I got recruited right after school. My teeth don't look the same due to dental braces. Spent most of my army years with the artillery at the Himalayan outskirts. My complexion changed but not my memories and dreams. I did pursue higher studies; completed my Master's degree by correspondence. You told me I could be a writer if I chose to," he said, sitting down beside her. SS took his most recent volume of poetry out of his attaché. "See, I've dedicated this book to you."

Priya looked closely at his eyes. They were familiar pools of brown and white from long ago. "I believe we know each other. Did you have to travel far to find me?"

"Took me three and half days to get here but I waited for this meeting for the past two decades.'

"Well, then I can make you a cup of tea at home. Let's go."

SS helped his favourite teacher up and they began walking in the direction of the nearest house, which was indeed that of Priya.

"Why is it that we couldn't find each other in all these years, SS?"

"Ma'am, you remember Udit, who was my best friend from middle school? I told him something. It was about how I felt towards you. He was the one who dissuaded me and said I shouldn't contact and disturb you. You were my dream lady. You told my parents about the first girl on whom I had a teenage crush because you thought it was affecting my studies. Within one month, we broke up because she responded to a wealthy admirer who showered her with gifts. I found solace in your sweet smile and the reassurance that, once I was employed, my true love would find me. I wished that my soulmate would be a splitting image of you. Yes, I had fallen in love with you over our two years together and never overcame those feelings in the times that followed."

"Utterly preposterous! I could never be that way with any student of mine. Not something befitting a third generation teacher. In my career as a schoolteacher and afterwards at University, there was a line that I never crossed with students."

"I do understand that, Ma'am. Yet, there was something different that I read in your eyes on the day we said goodbye after school. Many of the final classes and the farewell party were skipped due to my Cricket camp for the nationals."

"It was just affection and sadness, but I knew I had to let you go out in the world to make a place for yourself."

They stepped into her ancestral home, surrounded by coconut palms, a jackfruit tree, a couple of tamarind trees and plenty of plantains. The first photograph on the wall was that of Grandpa's army unit. Sahasranshu paused there to salute "his senior." Priya recalled that he still had the gaze, smile and tone of voice of his boyhood. He had truly been her favourite student though she would never admit this aloud; a teacher had to be impartial and could not afford to make the rest of the unruly class jealous.

"If you don't mind, I will make tea for the two of us."

"All right, SS. How is your family doing back home?"

"I am alone currently, Ma'am". Priya thought it best not to pry at that point. She placed the containers of dust tea and sugar, and the milk pot, on the kitchen slab. Saharanshu brewed the tea but Priya pointed out that tea dust would not take as long as tea leaves. They sipped tea and shared the whereabouts of mutual acquaintances. Mohit, who had been her student as well as neighbour in Delhi, now had his own Chartered accountancy firm. The Physics teacher settled in the United Kingdom where her sons were working. Later, when Priya relapsed into silence, she dozed off in her armchair.

SS watched her sleeping peacefully and found contentment in her presence. He thought it inexplicable that her face was the first that had come to mind as he was falling off a cliff during combat in Assam. If Ma'm asked how he overcame the trauma, he would reply that Nature helped him sometimes to remember and at other times to forget. Often birds, insects, flowers and rivers reminded him of Priya, if only in the context of poetry they had read together in class. Ultimately, Mother Nature embodied his abiding love.

After half an hour, Priya woke up. Her face wore an inscrutable expression as she asked, "Do I know you, young man?"

CHAPTER TWENTY-EIGHT

What will I do with What I Learn?

Madhumita Chanda

As I pushed the door lightly and walked into the half-lit room with spotlights sliding down the contours of the formidable members of the selection committee, my heart skipped a beat. Wait, you are a part-time teacher in an elite Govt. College, and have been successfully mentoring undergraduate and postgraduate students. You shouldn't be nervous. I tried to recentre my timid thoughts, misting the answers I was afraid to ask.

To my relief, the interviewers were kind and strangely polite. Among them, one pointed to the B.Ed. Degree enlisted in my CV and asked, "We also have a school which is the best in the whole of Bengal. Why didn't you apply to our school before?" Courses in English and Geography echoed from a disconcerting forgotten world. "As I am teaching in a degree College, so I thought...." my voice trailed off. A lady in the corner pitched in. "Have you taught Values and Ethics before?" Did I make a mistake while mailing my job application? I wondered. No, I was pretty sure. The vacancy was for an English teacher. "Well, we have enough English faculty. We are on the lookout for someone who would be able to teach Human values." She concluded authoritatively.

Looking into her eyes, I said, "Give me a week, and I believe I would be able to handle the subject."

I was surprised at my audacity. Just shut up. I warned myself.

"Don't be a fool. Tell her you cannot. You haven't even heard of this subject." The rational me pleaded.

By then, I had moved away from the men and women seated in the tastefully decorated room and was climbing the wall of lost time.

I saw the majestic school building, long corridors with spacious classrooms, and a well-curated garden with bunches of roses and jasmine lazing under the old sun. 7 March 2003. It was the first day of the new academic session. After the brief orientation program, we went to the teachers' room for refreshments. The concluding remark of the Father was still ringing in my ears. "Train your mind to see the invisible. There is an elephant in front of the students, which the teachers fail to see. It is only visible to the students. This restricts the teaching and learning process." His eyes lit up with a warm smile.

The sound of approaching footsteps broke my reverie. It was the teacher coordinator. She shoved a piece of paper into my hand. Honestly, for teachers, the eagerness for the new timetable is in no way less than the students. My eyes darted from one period to the next. Did I see correctly? I rubbed my eyes and peered into the small square box. Yes, I was to teach Geography to Class IX E students. A cold shiver ran down my spine. I was from a CBSE Board school, and this school was affiliated with the ICSE Board. The syllabus was so different from what I had studied in school. I liked geography, but what we had as a subject was Social Studies. It was an interesting smattering of history, geography, and civics clubbed into one.

I had established my credentials as a decent English teacher. If I teach geography now, it will ruin everything. Unlike the recess bell, the warning bell rang loud and clear.

I went to the library and flipped through the geography book. My head reeled at the sight of it. Apart from topographical maps, there were some mathematical problems! One has to calculate the location of a place with the help of longitudes and latitudes! I froze when I looked at the exercise at the end of the chapter. One sample question read like this.

'Imagine that you live in Lucknow located at 82° East. Your friend lives in London located at 0° GMT. It is noon in Lucknow now. Calculate the local time in London.'

The question stared back at me with all the unkindness in the world!

I prayed to God, my saviour. Did I sin? I had given up science for fear of all these mindless calculations, which always culminated in public disgrace and humiliation. I saw the invisible elephant! Why couldn't they? Why do people assume that if one pursued the Arts stream, one could teach any subject that falls within its ambit?

I plucked up my sagging spirit and walked into the Principal's office. " Sir, I can teach geography to Std VII students but not Std IX. I want to be honest with you. I cannot take up something I don't even know." I blurted out. The Principal looked at me kindly. God has finally listened to my prayers. I thought. I had hardly closed my eyes to say a small prayer when I looked up with disbelief. His voice belied the emotions. " I appreciate your honesty, but I can't help you much. Please follow the routine and take your allotted classes." "But Sir, they will laugh at me....tears welled up in my unsure eyes."

"All right. Since you insist, at least take your class for a month. I will ask your class about your performance, and if I find that you have failed in your endeavour, I shall alot someone else."

My joy knew no bounds. I could hear those watery noises freedom makes!

One month went by like an aeon.

With spring in my steps, I went up to meet the Principal. He looked up from a half-open file. "Congratulations, Madhumita! You have done an excellent job. Students are extremely pleased with you, and so am I."

My mouth fell open.

And sanity sat at the doorway, watching the world go by! "How?" "Why?" I could mumble two words in inaudible whispers. My elaborate scheme collapsed like the house of cards.

"I had called the class representative the day before yesterday and instructed him to collect feedback from the class about your competency in teaching geography. He told me you were good at it as you did not know the subject well!"

Oxymoron of some kind, huh! I did not know how to respond. The observation in itself was so difficult to process. I decided to get to the bottom of it.

I went to the staff room and asked the class representative to report to me immediately. Samiur Rehman, the CR, was a slender boy with delicate features and a well-mannered and quiet child. He came and stood before me, eyes fixed on the ground. But I was beside myself with anger and frustration. "Did you or did you not tell the Principal that I have taught the subject well and I did not know the subject? What on earth do you mean?" I asked him in a stern voice.

He looked up once. His liquid brown eyes made my heart melt. " Yes, Madam. When Sir asked me about you, I told him you taught us well. It is not me, the entire class feels so." In a small voice, he continued, " We all could see the effort you made to explain the contour maps and solve all the mathematical problems in the class. Those who know never tried enough to explore the concepts. Rather they indirectly encouraged us to go to them for tuition. Since you did not have an in-depth understanding of the terms and principles of Geography in detail, you first prepared the lesson plans meticulously and came to the class to deliver them."

This observation which was never an answer, rippled through my world like the sounds of a huge gong and quietened at finding itself chronicling my life.

How did...I mean... how did they know I was reading the textbook and solving all the problems from the exercises before rushing to school? Children are so insightful! Even if they remain quiet, they see through all the dubious facades we erect before them. The spectre of fear silences the voices but never the minds.

I also understood that even if one has not done something before, or is new to something doesn't necessarily mean, one can never. Samiur taught me to foray into unheard-of territories with confidence. Since then, my professional trajectory has been remarkably unique. I moved from Dhanbad to Kolkata. I was asked if I could join a college as a part-time teacher to teach postgraduate students in the Department of English. (I had been awarded a PhD degree by then). My answer was "Yes". It was a huge leap from secondary school to PG Dept. of English. Nevertheless, the sinking feeling in my stomach and dread and fear at the sight of stalwarts of academia made me sick with anxiety. I believe anxiety comes when we have fallen out of line with who we are. And I have allowed the mind to run the show. I reasoned with myself. Perhaps we listen to negative messages that the mind can produce and believe them to be the truth. But again, my students were proved right. I could smoothly fit myself into the mould of a professor from a high school teacher. And in both cases with zero experience!

There is a kind of infirmity in the human mind which relentlessly urges it to toss silks of life like a spider, weaving that net where the weight of the unknown thumps against the sky.

"Are you sure, you will be able to teach this subject?" I turned to look at her impatient face. "Yes, I can". I felt my way back, chasing the new growth of grass, in a faraway unknown field.

CHAPTER TWENTY-NINE

In Their Love, I Live

Shoma Elizabeth Francis

In a house where childhood dreams took flight,
I stood by plants and chairs in quiet delight.
A cane in hand, a wall of green,
Turned into a blackboard, a teacher unseen.
Imagination sparked, a passion unfurled,
In those early days, I taught a silent world.

My father's cane, once a tool of reprimand,
Became my sceptre in a kingdom unplanned.
With no students near, I taught the air,
Chairs were my pupils, plants listened with care.
Though chastised for the wall I marred,
The call to teach was etched in my heart, hard.

Years later, in classrooms filled with light,
I found myself guiding, with hope burning bright.
My journey began where young minds grew,
Their eager love made my spirit anew.
But it was in college, with students so dear,
That I truly felt love's tender cheer.

At twenty-three, with dreams in stride,

I entered the halls where I would abide.
Once stern with a frown, I chided with might
Then walked to my home in the dimming light

With bags in my grasp, I stepped outside
To find my students, waiting wide-eyed.
They ran to my side with hands reaching wide,
Grabbing my bags with contrite eyes.

As I quickened my pace, they followed besides,
With heartfelt apologies and beaming with pride.
Their laughter and gestures turned evening to light,
Their thoughtful embrace made my sternness take flight.

In their gleeful faces, I found my true light,
A bond filled with love, pure and bright.
For in their eyes, a joy I did see,
A teacher's true treasure: their love for me

The colleagues too, with kindness so rare,
Embraced me warmly, with genuine care.
In that place, I wasn't just a guide,
But a cherished soul, on every side.
In every lesson, in every face,
I found my purpose, my sacred place.

Now, I look back on those tender years,
With fond memories, laughter, and tears.
For in the life of a teacher, love leads the way,
In every word, in every day.
The blackboard may fade, the chalk may break,
But the hearts we touch are the marks we make.

For it's because of them that I truly live,
Their smiles, their trust, the joy they give.

They are my source, my endless delight,
In their love, I find my guiding light.
Through their hearts, my spirit does rise,
In their love, my purpose lies.

CHAPTER THIRTY

From Dolls to Dreams

Jeena Shaji

Once, there was a little girl who believed she was born to teach. Her days were spent in a tiny classroom of her own making, where dolls sat obediently in rows, and her voice, small but firm, filled the air with lessons from her imagination. A chalkboard, fashioned from whatever she could find, stood as the centerpiece of her world. It was in these moments that she felt most alive, most herself.

Even before she turned three, she was already trying to run alongside the neighbourhood kids on their way to school, her tiny feet struggling to keep up. But in her heart, she was already there—in the classroom, the place where she knew she was meant to be.

As she grew, so did her love for teaching. School became her sanctuary and her dream grew wings day by day. Every lesson she learnt, every teacher she admired, added another layer to her desire to stand in front of a real classroom one day. Her English teachers, in particular, became her idols. Their words were like seeds, planting themselves in the fertile soil of her mind, growing into a deep love for the language. She thrived in every competition—English Elocution, Recitation, Poetry Writing—her passion translating into success as naturally as the seasons change.

Teacher's Day was her annual moment of magic. On that day, she wasn't just a student; she became the teacher, walking in the very shoes of those she admired the most. For a few precious hours, she taught her juniors, and in doing so, she felt the thrill of stepping closer to her dream. At home, she would drape her mother's shawl like a saree, transforming herself once more. She'd gather her friends around, teaching them with the ease and joy of someone who knew that every lesson shared was also a lesson learned. In those moments, the line between her childhood play and her future blurred, like the soft edges of a dream just within reach, yet never quite as simple as it seemed.

When the time came to choose her path, it seemed only natural to follow her English teacher's advice and pursue a degree in Communicative English. She walked into college with her heart set on becoming a teacher, believing that this was the path she was destined to follow.

But life has a way of painting over our dreams with the dull colours of reality. As time passed, she began to see the cracks in her vision. Teaching, she realized, was not just a calling but a profession fraught with financial struggles. It was a path meant for those who were either well-off or willing to make do with less. Her dream began to fade, and she found herself letting go, bit by bit, of the future she had so carefully crafted in her mind.

During her internship interview, she and her friend were asked about their aspirations. The friend without a second thought said she wanted to pursue a PhD and become a teacher. She, however, reluctantly spoke of a different vision—one where she would take an MBA and become an HR Manager. At that moment, neither of them could have known that life was quietly rewriting their stories, switching their dreams in a way neither could foresee.

She was soon recruited by Infosys Bangalore, where she chose the stability of a career in HR over the uncertainty of teaching. It was a safe choice, one that offered financial security and the prestige of attending IIM. Yet, despite this, the flame of her first love—teaching—continued to flicker. She found a small piece of her dream in her role on the induction training team, where she could still teach, even if it was in a different capacity.

But life, unpredictable as ever, threw her another curve. Complications during pregnancy forced her to pause her IIM classes. For a while, things seemed to stabilize, but then the recession hit. She was called back to work, and with her baby in her arms, she returned, juggling the heavy load of her job, studies, and home life. The pressure was immense, like a storm that refused to let up. Then came the day when her baby needed surgery, and her world came to a standstill. She knew where her priorities lay. Her career was put on hold, and she became a full-time mother.

For nearly a year, she devoted herself entirely to her child. But the dream she had nurtured since childhood refused to die. As her baby grew stronger, so did her resolution to return to her studies. And as if the universe had been waiting for this moment, everything began to fall into place. She completed her master's, pursued a PhD, and finally, after all the detours, she stepped into the role she had always dreamed of—she became a teacher.

Now, she stands in front of a classroom, not of dolls, but of eager, bright-eyed students. Teaching may not bring the wealth that other careers do, but it fills her with a sense of accomplishment, a deep joy that no amount of money could ever buy. Every day, she experiences the profound satisfaction of guiding young minds through the beauty of a poem or the depth of a story. The joy she feels when she sees the light of understanding in their eyes is indescribable, a reward greater than any she could have imagined.

The girl who once draped her mother's shawl like a saree, who taught her dolls in a makeshift classroom, has finally stepped into her dream. Today, she wears a real saree, and her students are no longer just toys lined up in a row. And there is no greater privilege than leading them toward their tomorrows.

CHAPTER THIRTY-ONE

Teaching Wisdom: A Journey Through Quotes

Bibin Sebastian

On a quiet September morning, the corridors of St. Mary's School echoed with the excited whispers of students preparing for the Teachers' Day celebration. The walls, adorned with colourful posters and hand-drawn portraits, bore witness to the deep respect and admiration the students held for their teachers.

In one corner of the school, Mrs. Verma, the beloved history teacher, stood before the mirror in the staff room, adjusting her saree. She was known for her gentle demeanour and the ability to bring history to life, making her students see beyond the dates and events to understand the stories of people and civilizations. Today, as she prepared to attend the special assembly, she thought back to her first day as a teacher, decades ago, when she was as nervous as the students she was about to teach.

As she recollected, she smiled at the memory of her mentor, Mr. Sharma, who had once told her, "The whole art of teaching is only the art of awakening the natural curiosity of young minds for the purpose of satisfying it afterwards." Those words had stayed with her throughout her career, guiding her approach to teaching. She had always believed that her role was not just to impart knowledge but to spark curiosity, to make her students question, explore, and seek answers.

The assembly began with the students' choir singing a heartfelt tribute to the teachers, followed by a series of performances. The highlight of the event was a speech by Arjun, a final-year student who had always been shy but had shown remarkable growth over the years.

Arjun stepped up to the microphone, his voice slightly trembling. He began, "Today, as we celebrate Teachers' Day, I stand here not just as a student but as someone whose life has been profoundly shaped by the guidance of my teachers. I remember a quote by W.B. Yeats that perfectly captures the essence of education. He said, 'Education is not the filling of a pail, but the lighting of a fire.' This fire, this passion for learning, was ignited in me by teachers like Mrs. Verma, who made me see history not as a series of events but as a living, breathing entity that shapes our present and future."

The students applauded, and Mrs. Verma felt a warmth spread through her heart. She had seen Arjun struggle with his self-confidence, and today, he stood before the entire school, speaking with conviction. She knew that this was the true reward of teaching—not the grades, not the accolades, but the transformation of a student into a confident, curious individual.

Arjun continued, "I've learned that good teaching is not about giving the right answers but about asking the right questions, as Josef Albers, the artist and educator, once said. Mrs. Verma taught me that history is not just about knowing what happened, but about understanding why it happened, and how those events still influence us today. She encouraged me to ask questions, to dig deeper, and to find connections between the past and the present."

As Arjun spoke, Mrs. Verma's thoughts drifted to the many students she had taught over the years. She remembered each one—some eager to learn, others struggling to find their path. She recalled a time when she had to console a student who had failed a major exam. She had told him, "Your mistakes end the moment you find a good teacher," echoing the words of Dr. A.P.J. Abdul Kalam.

She knew that failure was not the end but the beginning of a new journey of learning and growth.

Arjun's speech took a personal turn as he shared a story from his childhood. "When I was younger, I didn't really understand the importance of education. It was just something I had to do because my parents said so. But one day, my teacher told me something that changed my perspective. She said, 'Education is not preparation for life; education is life itself.' Those words by John Dewey stayed with me, and I began to see education not as a chore, but as an opportunity to explore the world and to understand my place in it."

Mrs. Verma could see the heads nodding in the audience. The students were engaged, listening intently to Arjun's words. She felt a deep sense of fulfilment, knowing that she had played a part in shaping these young minds.

Arjun then shared a quote by Rabindranath Tagore, "The primary purpose of teaching is not to provide explanations but to open the doors of the mind to thought." He added, "This is exactly what my teachers have done for me. They didn't just give me answers; they encouraged me to think, to question, and to explore. And that, I believe, is the true purpose of education."

As Arjun concluded his speech, he quoted Malala Yousafzai, saying, "One child, one teacher, one book, and one pen can change the world." He looked at the audience and said, "Each of us has the power to make a difference, and it all begins with the education we receive and the teachers who guide us. So, today, I want to thank all my teachers for believing in me, for challenging me, and for lighting the fire of curiosity in me."

The hall erupted in applause as Arjun stepped down from the stage. Mrs. Verma wiped a tear from her eye, overwhelmed by the emotion of the moment. She knew that teaching was not just a profession but a calling, a responsibility to shape the future.

After the assembly, as the teachers gathered in the staff room, the conversations were filled with laughter and memories. Mr. Kapoor, the science teacher, shared a story about one of his former students who had gone on to become a renowned scientist.

"Wherever you find something extraordinary, you'll find the fingerprints of a great teacher," he quoted Arne Duncan, his face beaming with pride.

Mrs. Verma reflected on the diverse experiences shared by her colleagues. She realized that teaching was not just about delivering lessons but about imparting values, as Roger Moore had said, "Teach love, generosity, good manners, and some of that will drift from the classroom to the home, and who knows, the children will be educating the parents." She had always believed in this philosophy and had seen its impact on her students over the years.

As the day ended, Mrs. Verma walked through the empty corridors of the school, her mind filled with the day's events. She thought of Mahatma Gandhi's words, "The most important textbook for students is the teacher." She knew that beyond the textbooks, it was the teacher's passion, dedication, and love for the subject that truly influenced the students.

She also recalled Bill Gates' words, "Technology is just a tool. In terms of getting the kids working together and motivating them, the teacher is the most important." In this age of digital learning, she knew that her role as a teacher was more crucial than ever. It was her responsibility to guide her students, to motivate them, and to help them navigate the vast sea of information available to them.

Finally, as she locked her classroom door, Mrs. Verma thought of Nelson Mandela's words, "Education is the most powerful weapon which you can use to change the world." She felt a deep sense of pride and purpose. She knew that every lesson she taught, every word of encouragement she gave, was contributing to a better future.

As she stepped out into the evening, the sun setting in the horizon, she smiled, thinking of the quote by William Arthur Ward, "The mediocre teacher tells. The good teacher explains. The superior teacher demonstrates. The great teacher inspires." She hoped that in her years of teaching, she had been more than just a teller of facts, but an inspirer of dreams.

Walking towards the school gate, she remembered Scott Hayden's words, "Teachers have three loves: love of learning, love of learners, and the love of bringing the first two loves together." Mrs. Verma knew that these three loves had guided her throughout her career, and they would continue to do so in the years to come.

As she left the school, Mrs. Verma knew that her journey as a teacher was far from over. For her, teaching was not just a job but a lifelong mission to light the fire of curiosity, to open the doors of the mind, and to inspire the next generation to change the world, one student at a time.

CHAPTER THIRTY-TWO

Be a Wise Teacher

Thomas A Mattappallil

Being naïve and a first-generation learner, its
difficult in the initial days and years to survive in
a noble profession like teaching, especially to exist
in a country like India, where salaries are lower and respect is
low.

Pressures from society, family, and cousins to clear NET
And PhD, but never looks into the candidate's passion
To reach greater heights. For them, it's just 'Speaking',
Do not demean them as someone without any value.

Understand teachers! live with their sound, Not just that,
But with a huge amount of preparation and qualities like
remembering,
Creativity, improvisation, critical, and analytical skills
Of things observed to deliver a meaningful sentence in the
class.

Intense reading makes them insightful.
Without shame, they share updated knowledge,
Beyond this, they learn subjects unknown to them.
Hello! Society, do not judge teachers with your

False beliefs and prejudices, shared with you by those ignorant.

Sadly, some treat them with disdain.
Illiterates disrespect them.
Thinking they're unworthy of the minimal amount they're paid,
Yes! Maybe they're teachers without values, but do not judge
them.
With the yardstick of immoral values and monetary benefits.

Yes! Education, exposure, and being Wise matters for a teacher.
Alas! Some play cheap tricks, demeaning this profession.
They may survive momentarily, but it is not
Suitable for a teacher who aspires to learn and live with values.
For a teacher who wishes to be enlightened to educate others.

Novices in this profession may often hear
"I am Senior; you follow me closely, lest you be in danger."
Since you joined last, you have done everything according to
the seniors' wishes,
Who snatches away the credit for what you do?
Rather than commending you on your good initiatives.

It's the Great Indian Drama that is staged in this field, based on
'seniority and experience' though you have
more teaching experience to your credit as you join
a new institution, you are deemed to be 'junior'!
Ha! Ha! Ha! It's a serious Dhamaka and joke.
Which even the Great Indian 'Boards' had never thought about!

A teacher should initiate a silent revolution.
Like the Great Wiseman and philosophers in the world,
who shared curiosity to learn every time,
Learn from their wise professors.
And tries to enlighten a dark, ignorant world.

A teacher should be open to new knowledge
Show patience to contemplate everything seen in the world,
Question and respond to evils,
to make this world amiable for all.
A teacher spreads the words of wisdom
through experiences, anecdotes, and testimonies.
witnessed in texts and lives with an altruistic,
inclusive, and egalitarian attitude.

CHAPTER THIRTY-THREE

Nurturing Minds

Aswathy Balachandran

Being a teacher
I designed the fabric of my kids
in befitting colours.
Sitting in our garden
I proudly watched
those caterpillars
turning into butterflies.
We grew together and cherished
the process of becoming.

Now amidst those
Intriguing intelligences
I must skilfully operate
as an effective supplement.
Sitting in the snow-clad orchard
I still hope to kindle hearts
with such warmth and empathy
no machine can replace.

CHAPTER THIRTY-FOUR

Letter Expressing Gratitude to My Teacher

Keerthana Deepak

Dear Ma'am,

On this Teacher's Day, I would like to take the opportunity to express my heartfelt gratitude to you. Even now I remember the day you came to our class and gave us a motivational talk on 'how much you lose in life if you doubt to grab onto the opportunities presented to you'. Your insights left a profound impact on the shy, naive girl who was always afraid to try something new. To that unmotivated girl's bleak and dull life, you were like a beacon of hope which ignited a spark in that girl's heart which made her think that maybe it's not too late for her to-do what she wants. I was that girl, and I will ever be grateful to you for saving someone you needn't save.

There's a quote written by Mark Van Dover, which says, "the art of teaching is the art of assisting discoveries", and I truly believe that there are no truer words than these to describe your beautiful way of teaching. The way you taught always transcended the classroom and went beyond anything that could be contained in a mere textbook. You made learning all fun and every class of yours that I attended showed me a new perspective of life which I could have never thought of on my own. You realised the potential in me and never failed to nurture it. Your praises always boosted my confidence and made me believe that anything could be possible as long as one works hard for it. You helped me navigate through life the way that a compass guides a lost sailor through the rough seas. You helped me, not only in academics, but also in understanding the way of life. Your ever pleasant and calm demeanour never failed to make my day jubilant. You would always greet us with a warm smile and always explained every doubt no matter how many times we asked.

To me, you are not just a teacher, you are a mentor, an inspiration, an unwavering pillar of strength that always kept me going through thick or thin. You are an unforgettable part of my life and I'll be eternally grateful to you for moulding me into the person I'm today.

With intense love and respect,

Forever your student,

Keerthana Deepak